A Souvenir from Paris
and Other Stories

by

Maggie Rayner

A Souvenir from Paris and Other Stories

A SOUVENIR FROM PARIS

'Thanks, Melanie, that's great,' said the Ambassador, putting down the document I'd translated for him. He looked at me over the top of his reading glasses.

'Sorry you had to work over the weekend. Why don't you take the afternoon off? Make the most of this lovely September sunshine!'

'Thank you, I will!'

I left his office swiftly before he changed his mind. David, the Ambassador's Chief of Staff, glanced up at me from his computer as I passed his desk.

'Wish he'd let me go too! What are you going to do with yourself then, Mel?'

I thought for a moment. 'I'd like to do some painting. It's perfect weather to sit outside and sketch.'

'Of course…you're always painting. Well, enjoy yourself.'

I smiled, and as I turned to leave he added, 'if you want some company later a load of us are going to the Buddha Bar tonight - you're welcome to come along if you like.'

'I probably won't, but thanks anyway.'

I walked away down the corridor, feeling his eyes upon me. I knew he liked me – and to be honest I thought he was rather attractive, too - but I just wasn't ready for a workplace romance right now.

I took the Metro home to my apartment where I'd lived since taking up my post at the British Embassy in Paris, nearly two years ago. Moving here had been the best thing I'd ever done. Feeling low after splitting up with my long-term boyfriend, desperate to get away from London and do something new, I spotted the advert for a translator and knew this job was meant for me. Working in a foreign city, using my language skills, gave my confidence the boost it needed - the perfect way to get over a bad love affair. The bitterness and anger I'd felt when my ex walked out had gradually subsided, although I had to admit to a lingering fear of being hurt again, an unwillingness to risk getting involved with someone new.

My apartment was near the Eiffel Tower, and it was thrilling to live so close to the iconic landmark that had fascinated me since childhood. I'd arrived in Paris towards the end of 1999 so had been lucky enough to witness the Millennium celebrations, the breath-taking sight of the Tower adorned in a million twinkling lights and the eye-popping firework display as the new year began, full of excitement and hope.

I kicked off my shoes, took off my business suit and changed into shorts and a tee shirt, brushed my long, dark brown hair and tied it back into a ponytail. I glanced in the mirror, deciding I didn't look too bad, then collected my painting kit and left the apartment, enjoying the freedom of being out of the office on a Monday afternoon. Paris was looking lovely in the Autumn sunshine. I walked along the street lined with cars parked bumper to bumper, terraces with mansard roofs and wrought-iron balconies, feeling so lucky to be living in the famous capital, and crossed the busy road leading to the Champs de Mars, the large green space between the Eiffel Tower and the Ecole Militaire. I made my way along the straight gravel paths framing wide expanses of lawns and flower beds and settled on a spot in front of an avenue of pollarded trees beyond which the top two-thirds of the Tower rose into the cloudless blue sky. I sat down on a green metal bench, feeling the sun on my face and watching the passers-by: groups of tourists, local people walking their little dogs, joggers, mothers with toddlers in tow, Parisians and visitors alike gathering on the grass to picnic and relax in the warm weather.

The Tower was a challenging image to capture, its curves and wrought-iron lattice work familiar the world over, and every time I struggled to get it right. Balancing my sketchpad on my knees with a palette of watercolours beside me, I quickly outlined the Tower and the trees in pencil, then, dipping my brush in a jar of water, carefully painted the tall, straight trunks of the trees and their geometrically pruned branches. Next, I mixed pale shades of green and yellow for the leaves, and ochre and grey for the sandy, gravelly ground beneath. I could feel myself relaxing, fully immersed in my task, and was just about to tackle the most difficult part of the picture – the Tower itself - when from behind me came a penetrating female voice with an American accent.

'Gee! What a beautiful painting! I love the way you've done those trees!'

I stopped, my paint brush in mid-air.

'Sorry, I didn't mean to disturb you!' said the woman. 'Parlez-vous anglais?'

'It's okay, I'm English,' I said, turning to her.

'Thank goodness! That's all the French I know!'

The woman sat down heavily on the bench next to me.

'Gee, it's so hot today,' she said, fanning herself with her guidebook. 'I don't want to disturb you, please, carry on.'

As a painter you get used to people staring while you work. They usually get bored pretty quickly and go away; hopefully this woman would too.

'I just lurrrve Paris,' the woman continued. 'I'm with a tour group, but they've gone shopping this afternoon and I wanted to be outside in the sunshine. Do you live here?'

'Yes.'

'Oh my, how lovely – it's one of the most beautiful cities in the world. How long have you lived here?'

'Nearly two years.' I was reluctant to be drawn into conversation, but felt unable to ignore a direct question. I continued painting.

'I'm real thirsty, I'm gonna get myself a drink. Can I get you anything?'

'No thank you.'

I watched the woman as she ambled off towards one of the green-painted kiosks which sold drinks and snacks, her large hips rolling from side to side. After a few minutes she returned, carrying a can of cola and an ice cream, and resumed her seat. I was concentrating on my picture, trying to get the angle of the Tower's curvature just right. The woman finished her ice cream and said, 'I live in New York City. I adore it, it's home, but this place is something else.'

She took a slug of her drink. 'Have you been to the States?'

'Yes. I had a holiday in New York, just before I moved here. We visited all the sights, but…' I hesitated. I had already said too much.

'You sound disappointed.'

'Oh no, the place was amazing! It was the company that was bad…'

The woman nodded, wisely.

'They say it's not where you go that matters, but the person you're with. Take me for instance. All my married life I wanted to come to Europe, but my husband didn't want to travel – the furthest I ever got him was to Boston! He passed away four years ago, and since then I've been to London, and Rome, and now here I am in Paris! I travel with the tour group, so I'm not on my own. I've had the best time! But everything I look at, I wish my husband was there to see it with me.'

'It must have taken some courage, for you to start travelling abroad.'

'I guess it did. But it's been the best way to help me move on. My son tells me I'm doing the right thing. What is it he says? I'm becoming a 'eu-ro-phile'!' She clapped her hands on her knees and laughed. 'He's a good boy. He's done all his lawyer training now and he's having an interview tomorrow for a job with a big financial corporation. I'm so proud of him! Do you have children?'

'God no. I don't even have a husband!'

'Aaah…something to do with the 'bad company'?'

'It just didn't work out, that's all.'

'So, what happened, honey?'

The woman's tone softened with a concern that I found hard to resist. Maybe this confessional, tell-all American approach had its merits? Holding my paintbrush to one side I took a deep breath and began.

'We – my ex-boyfriend and I - booked a holiday in New York. We stayed at a good hotel, took the Circle Line cruise around

Manhattan, went up the Empire State Building, saw all the sights – but all the time it felt as if he wasn't really there, as if he was thinking about something – or someone – else. Then on our last day he took me up to the top of the World Trade Center. I remember standing on the observation deck, it was a beautiful day, the sky was the clearest blue and the view was fantastic. I was so naïve – I thought he was going to ask me to marry him – but he didn't. When we got home he told me he was leaving, to 'give himself some space' – and within a week he'd shacked up with another girl. I was devastated.'

The woman shook her head, full of sympathy.

'You poor thing - I can see that hurt at the time. But I'm telling you, it sounds to me like you're better off without him! And you've done well, picking up your life, coming here.'

I looked at her kind face, lined with years of cares and worries. She had heard my story many times before.

'Thank you. But I still find it hard at times. And it spoilt my dreams of New York!'

'Next time make sure you go there with the right person! You've just got to go out there and find them. One day you'll be old and fat like me, honey, so do it now! Take the risk!'

I laughed, already feeling better for telling my story to this complete stranger.

'Well, if you put it like that…'

I knew she was right; it was what my friends had been telling me for ages, but I hadn't been listening.

In a renewed state of mind I returned to my work, steadied my hand, and carefully painted the structure at the very top of the Tower. My task complete, I put down my paintbrush and held my sketchpad at arms' length to examine my picture. I'd captured the curvature of the Tower exactly right; the trees were a pleasing shape and colour, there was life and light in the painting and the composition was good. It was the best I'd ever done. In that moment I felt my spirit lighten; that last knot of resentment I'd carried for so long unravelled and disappeared. I experienced a feeling of relief, of resolution, a readiness to move on. And, I decided, I would go to the Buddha bar tonight.

After a pause, the woman, thinking of home, said, 'that's where my son's going tomorrow, for his interview, the World Trade Center. I do hope he gets the job – to think that when I look across the water from Queens, he'll be working up there in the Twin Towers. His father would be so proud.'

'I wish him every success.'

I held up my painting to show her.

'It's beautiful! Well done. I've so enjoyed talking to you today.'

'Me too.'

I suddenly knew what I had to do.

'Here, take it, it's yours.'

Carefully, I tore the page from my sketchpad.

'Oh, I couldn't possibly!'

'No, I insist. A souvenir from Paris. Just one more thing…'

I always sign and date my work. I took my thinnest brush, and carefully wrote in the bottom left-hand corner:

Mel Jones 10th September 2001

'Here you are. And I hope your son gets on well tomorrow!'

THE LAST DROP

Bath, 1946

Clive Best met Angela, his future wife, one Spring morning at a bus stop in Larkhall, in the east of Bath. An unassuming man of slight build with brown hair and hazel eyes, Clive was a clerk with Bath Insurance Company, having resumed his job after being de-mobbed from the Army. He lived quietly with his widowed mother in a small terraced house and had no romantic ambitions, so when the striking woman with shoulder-length fair hair caught his eye he was surprised and rather flattered. She smiled at him and they talked about the weather; he noticed that she was wearing trousers. She sat next to him on their journey into the city centre and as they travelled past bomb sites, relics of the Bath Blitz of '42, she told him she was called Angela and lived in a bedsit in Larkhall. An ex-Land Girl, who had lost her parents in the war, she now worked for the Council in the parks department. They took the bus together for the rest of the week and come Friday he was plucking up the courage to ask her out when she said, 'there's a good film on at the Beau Nash tomorrow. Would you like to take me?'

As they got to know each other Clive realised that Angela enjoyed wearing the trousers in more senses than one. It was she who decided where they should go and what they should do, and she who, towards Christmas, suggested they get married. Clive's colleagues teased him, saying, 'at least you'll have an easy life, Clive – all you'll ever have to say is, 'yes Angela!' and 'no Angela!' He took their comments in his stride, being sufficiently self-aware to know that he was swapping one dominating woman – his mother – for another. But it suited him, and he loved his fiancée, admiring her strong character and physical strength. At thirty, she was two years older than him and two inches taller, a perfect match as far as he was concerned. As for Angela, she saw Clive as a reliable sort with a reasonable wage who had potential and would do her bidding: she liked small men that she could dominate.

Clive's mother and Angela did not get on, so Clive left home and the newly-weds rented a flat while they saved up to buy a house. After three years of marriage with no children to show for it, Angela went for tests at the hospital, to be informed that she was infertile. Shocked, but not overly upset, she and Clive decided to enjoy their lives child-free and concentrate on their careers. Clive soon gained promotion to Claims Officer, while Angela developed her horticultural skills, building on her experience as a Land Girl and working in Bath's parks.

Angela was keen that they should better themselves, and when Clive's mother died she seized the opportunity, using Clive's inheritance to put a good deposit on a three-storey Georgian townhouse on a hill in Widcombe, a pleasant area of Bath, close to the river Avon and the city centre. They moved in and busied themselves decorating, making it their own, Angela seeing it as a good place from which to launch her ambitions.

They paid little attention to their new neighbours and barely noticed the disabled young man who lived in the house opposite, sitting by the window in his wheelchair with a ringside view into their lives…

From my chair by the window on the first floor of my home in Widcombe, facing north I can see the hills surrounding Bath in the distance and can just make out the roof of the Abbey. Coming closer, I watch the comings and goings in the road, people on their way to work and school and returning home at the end of the day. It gives me an interest as I have little else to do. I was in good health until the age of twenty-one. At first there was a numbness in my feet which progressed to my legs and slowly crept up my body, then into my arms and hands, and by the age of twenty-three I could feel nothing from the neck down and lost the power of speech. The medics still can't explain why this happened or what my illness is called, but if there's no cure the fact it doesn't have a name is irrelevant. I just have to live with it.

So, here I am, aged twenty-five, living at home with my widowed father and my carer, Mrs Bird. My older sister dotes on me when she comes to visit and I enjoy seeing my niece and nephew, although what they make of poor old Uncle Martin sat there dribbling with his tongue lolling out, God knows. I hope one day they'll understand and at least be tolerant of people who are different.

Mrs Bird takes care of my day-to-day needs. She is well-meaning, and talks to me constantly, having been told that I might be able to hear, even if I can't respond. Sometimes we sit and listen to the wireless, giving us both a rest. She keeps me up-to-date with the news, and feeds me brown gunge through a tube, saying, 'be a good boy, Martin, and drink it up to the last drop!' As if I have a choice in the matter.

I observe the regulars – the postie, the butcher's delivery boy on his bicycle, travelling salesmen - and I keep an eye on the neighbours - they'd be surprised at how much I know about their routines, and their secrets. Yes, I've seen the gas man chatting up the housewives while their husbands are out at work, inspecting more than just their meters…

A new couple in their thirties moved into the house opposite a few weeks ago. They probably don't realise but I can see right into their drawing room on the first floor – they really should get some net curtains. He looks an ordinary sort of chap – works in insurance, Mrs Bird reckons – but his wife is more interesting, a big-built, bossy-looking woman. I wonder who they are?

Angela left the employ of the Council to venture out on her own, setting up her own garden design business. She relished the challenge, and soon she received her first commission, to create a colourful border and a pond at a house on Combe Down. When she enlisted Clive to help her with the groundworks at the weekends he protested, telling her he'd been working all week, and she gave him an earful.

'You call that work, sitting behind a desk all day? I'm trying to set up a successful business here. The least you can do is come and help me out!'

Clive returned to the office on Monday morning, exhausted, saying he hadn't done so much digging since he was in the Army. His colleagues ribbed him about his wife's venture, but he was proud of her and told them so.

'My Angela's a clever girl. She knows a lot about gardening and there's nothing wrong with using your expertise.'

'And who's cleaning the house and cooking the dinner?'

'We take turns, if you must know.'

The men doubled up in laughter.

'Wouldn't work in my house!' declared one of them, 'why have a dog and bark yourself?!'

Mrs Bird is watching the house opposite where Mrs Best has just closed the front door and is walking down the hill, wearing an oversized white shirt tucked into her trousers and carrying an artist's portfolio case.

'There she goes - off to meet a client, I suppose. She's set herself up in some fancy job — I saw her advert in the paper.'

Mrs Bird gets up to fetch the Bath & Wilts Chronicle from her bag.

I'll read it to you. Listen to this:

'Angela Best, garden designer. Do you need help organising your outside space? Ask the expert! Paving, water features, planting – let me bring a piece of paradise to your home!'

'Paradise indeed! All you need is a bit of lawn and a vegetable patch! Still, she must be attracting some work, she always seems to be busy. I feel sorry for her husband though – yesterday I saw him putting the vacuum cleaner round! Talk about under the thumb...'

I have also observed Mr Best doing the housework. The other day he was cleaning the large window in the drawing room and glanced out, noticing me for the first time. He stopped, the cloth in his hand, and stared at me for a moment, then looked away and resumed his work.

Word spread, and as more commissions came in Angela needed to employ a full-time assistant and buy a van to transport her gardening equipment. She and Clive had insufficient savings, so Angela made an appointment to see their bank manager to ask for a loan. She returned home, furious.

'He refused me! He said they don't make loans to women! He wants to see YOU!'

Clive duly went to the bank, but they were only prepared to lend a fraction of what Angela had asked for, and made the loan to him, not her.

'I'm going to need more than that, and if the bank won't provide, then you'll have to step up to the mark,' Angela told him. 'You must work harder, Clive – get yourself promoted!'

Things are moving apace in the house opposite. Mrs Best has bought a van with 'Angela Best – garden design' written on the side, and she goes out in it most days. Mrs Bird is surprised how well the business is taking off, wondering who can afford such luxuries around here. Must be part of the post-war building boom, she reckons.

Today, I saw Mr Best return home with a bunch of flowers. He must have brought good news as he was rewarded with a kiss, and Mrs Best poured drinks for them both. Then they had an early night because she led him upstairs to the bedroom and drew the curtains before it was dark…

Angela was delighted when her husband was made Senior Claims Officer and decided it was time he increased his (and, by association, her) social standing, in keeping with his new position. She suggested he join the Masons.

'But you can't just turn up,' said Clive, 'you have to be invited.'

'So, find someone to invite you! You must know someone who's a member!'

Asking the not-so-subtle question around his office, Clive discovered that several of his colleagues were indeed Masons. He made the right noises and after a suitable length of time was initiated into the Bath Lodge of the secret society in a ceremony at the Masonic Hall, a short walk from home.

'It's not a secret society,' he was told, 'it's a society with secrets.'

Angela was pleased. As a woman she was excluded from many of the city's institutions where businessmen gathered to build a network of useful contacts, but she intended to use Clive as her proxy. It suited him, too - he found that he enjoyed the company of his fellow-men and enthusiastically supported the organisation's charitable activities, whilst at the same time plugging Angela's business, as she directed. Angela herself happily participated in Ladies

Nights, speaking to the men as well as their wives, using the opportunity for self-publicity.

'You've got quite a woman there!' remarked one of the members to Clive, 'gutsy and good-looking too! Be careful or she'll wear you out!'

Clive was growing used to such remarks and brushed them off with a smile, putting it down to jealousy.

Business boomed, and the couple's combined wages allowed them a comfortable lifestyle. They started giving parties, entertaining contacts with drinks and laughter, and Angela's order book was overflowing, rather like the bottle of champagne that she was pouring out to her guests.

'There you are, Clive,' she said, emptying the dregs into her husband's glass, 'you can have the last drop!'

It's two years since the Best's moved in, and apart from a cursory 'good morning' they've never spoken to my father or Mrs Bird – they're only interested in potential customers, and don't bother with us or the other neighbours. Mr Best glances over at me occasionally, with curiosity, then gets embarrassed and looks away. I thought things were going well for them, but lately I've noticed the couple arguing. Take this morning, for instance – I could see her, jabbing her finger at him and shouting, then he left the house, slamming the door behind him, and walked away carrying his briefcase, looking downtrodden. Mrs Best made herself comfortable in a chair by the window and lit a cigarette. Later, I watched her leave the house, off to another appointment. I hope she treats her clients more gently than she does her husband…

Angela was unhappy. She'd been riding on success, but other rivals were starting up in garden design, undercutting her, and she'd recently lost a couple of potential orders. Moreover, Clive wasn't pulling his weight. Instead of relishing the responsibilities of his higher position at work he was getting stressed by it and had developed an ulcer which made him difficult to live with.

'I'm sorry, Angela, I'm not well,' he told her, clutching his stomach as a wave of nausea washed over him. 'The doctor said I should slow down a bit…'

'Well, I'm not having that! You mustn't rest until you're Head of Claims!'

'But Angela, you don't understand…I'm not cut out for higher management – I can't cope with the pressure, the politics of it all. Quite frankly, I was happier as a clerk!'

'You're pathetic, Clive! You'll have to try harder! I want to move to a bigger house up Lansdown and we're going to need more money. I'm working all the hours I can and I expect you to do your share!'

The weeks went on with little improvement in Clive's condition. Angela felt he'd let her down, wasting the potential she thought he had, and now she found him dull and boring. He even disappointed her in the bedroom, rejecting her advances, saying he was too tired. She put her energy into her job, winning a new contract to install a water feature and rockery at a property in Weston, but remained frustrated at the state of her marriage.

One Ladies Night at the Masonic Hall she left Clive with his cronies and was standing at the bar, smoking and drinking, when one of the men sidled up to her. She found him attractive and started flirting with him, and he made her laugh with his patter and innuendos. Towards the end of the evening, he lowered his voice and said to her, 'actually, I could do with some advice about my red hot poker…'

She leaned towards him and replied, 'why don't you come round and see me?'

Now, this is interesting.

Recently, on certain afternoons while Mr Best is out at work, I've observed a professional type in a smart suit and tie, paying a visit to Mrs Best. He arrives in his Morris Minor, she lets him in, serves him drinks in the drawing room, then takes him upstairs — I watch her, closing the bedroom curtains. He stays for a couple of hours then leaves, with a surreptitious look. I'm surprised Mrs Bird hasn't noticed, but she often nods off after lunch so might not take it in like I do.

Of course, they could be discussing a future garden design project, but I can sniff adultery in the air. Does her husband know what's going on? I doubt it. And what would he do if he found out?

Angela felt alive again. Her old verve returned, business improved, and she took on another employee, allowing her to spend time at home for planning and paperwork - or so she told Clive. She lost patience with her husband's health problems and although she'd always enjoyed being the dominating force in their marriage, having a thrusting new lover was very exciting. She was sure Clive was oblivious to her affair, and didn't think anyone else would notice or care. After all, it wasn't as if someone was watching the house all day…

But rumours around the Lodge were rife.

One evening Clive attended a Masons' dinner and as the drink flowed he was aware of a couple of men glancing his way, smirking. He ignored them, but later, when he was in a cubicle in the Gents, he overheard the two saying:

'Did you see Clive's face? What a picture! He really has no idea, does he.'

'Poor sod. Embarrassing, isn't it.'

'Do you know what they've started calling him at the office? *Cuckold Clive*!"

The men erupted into laughter, leaving Clive in turmoil. After the dinner he walked home, looked in on his wife who was already asleep, and went to the spare room where he lay awake, pondering what to do. Was she really having an affair with one of his fellow-Masons? Had he neglected her to the point where she'd been forced to look elsewhere? Or was this the real Angela, cruel and selfish, who had used him and now cast him aside? He thought of his colleagues and friends, laughing at him behind his back, and felt humiliated, his self-esteem at rock-bottom. His mind was in a whirl and his stomach ached. He couldn't go on like this. There was only one thing for it: tomorrow, he would confront her.

The following morning Clive left for work, not looking his wife in the eye. He planned to talk to her that evening, but the stress of it all played on his ulcer and come the afternoon he felt unwell, so asked the boss if he could go home. Approaching his house Clive saw a Morris Minor parked in the street; he'd noticed a similar model in the Lodge car park.

Clive swallowed the bitter heartburn which rose in the back of his throat, let himself in and climbed up to the first floor. Suddenly a figure, hitching up his trousers, pushed past him, ran down the stairs and rushed out the front door. In shock, Clive hurried up to the bedroom where his wife was sitting on the side of the bed in her underwear.

'So it's true! You *are* having an affair! Angela, how could you?'

'We got a bit carried away, that's all…Don't worry about it, Clive.'

'Don't worry? *Don't worry?!*'

The anger and resentment he had suppressed for years welled up inside him.

'I've been working myself to death to help you and your business! I've done everything you asked, and this is how you repay me!'

She laughed at him, scornfully.

'*You?! I'm* the one who's been doing all the *real* work. You'd be nothing without me!'

Clive advanced towards her, his heart racing. A voice shouted obscenities he hadn't heard since his Army days, and he realised it was his own.

'Clive! I didn't know you had it in you!' she said in surprise, taunting him, sniggering at his reddening face.

Something snapped. Clive moved quickly, and before Angela could dodge out of his way he had his hands around her throat, squeezing hard.

'Enough!' he cried, 'I can't stand it any longer! You've made me a laughing stock!'

Angela's eyes bulged as she fought for breath and she kicked out at him, managing to push him away. Fearful that her normally docile husband had flipped and there was no telling what he might do next, she ran down to the kitchen where she seized a knife to defend herself. Fuelled by his anger, Clive chased her, grabbed her from behind and they wrestled together, ending up in the drawing room where she fought back, holding the knife above her head, using her height to her advantage. He tried to disarm her, but as they struggled the pair lost their balance and Angela fell to the floor, bringing Clive down on top of her.

Good God, the Best's are having a fight! He must have confronted her about her lover – I saw a man rush out and drive away, just after Mr Best got home. But what's happening now? She's holding a knife above her head – I can see the blade, glinting in the light. I think she's going to stab him! But no – in their struggle, they've both fallen on the floor.

I'm willing Mrs Bird to wake up so that she can see what's happening, but she just sits there, asleep. I muster every force in my body to shout out, but I can't move or utter a sound.

Clive caught his breath and climbed off his wife, then looked in horror at her motionless, twisted body, her clothes dyed scarlet, the knife protruding from her stomach.

'Angela!' he cried, holding her, feeling for a pulse and finding none.

'Angela! Come back to me!'

But it was too late. She was dead.

Mr Best is standing there, as white as a sheet, looking at his hands which are red with blood. Then he stares out the window, his face an expression of horror and disbelief, and looks straight at me. Within minutes I hear a siren, and a police car and an ambulance draw up. Mrs Bird awakes with a start.

'What on earth's going on?'

She looks outside, watching as two policemen enter the Best's house, followed by the ambulance men. There's some activity in the drawing room but so many figures that we can't make out what's happening. The medics carry a covered stretcher into the ambulance and drive away, and shortly afterwards the police march a bloody, dishevelled Mr Best out of the house, in handcuffs.

Mrs Bird is beside herself.

'What's been happening? Did you see anything, Martin?' she asks me, frantically, knowing that I can't answer.

The next day a policeman visits us as part of house-to-house inquiries and comes over to the window where Mrs Bird and I are sitting.

'You had a ringside view!' he remarks.

'Yes, but I was asleep!' says Mrs Bird. 'I only woke up when I heard the siren, and the police and ambulance arrived. I still can't believe it - I mean, I've seen Mr and Mrs Best arguing, but I had no idea things might turn violent. He always seemed such a quiet sort.'

'And what about the young man?' asks the policeman, looking at me.

'Martin, he's called. Well, as you can see, officer, he's badly disabled. The doctors say he might be aware of what's going on, but we can't be sure. In any case, if he did see something, he wouldn't be able to tell you.'

Mrs Bird smooths my hair away from my forehead.

'Poor Martin, you don't even know what we're talking about, do you?'

At Bath police station the officer in charge of the investigation, Detective Inspector Todd, interviewed Clive, accompanied by his solicitor.

'I put it to you that you discovered your wife was having an affair, you attacked her with a knife and killed her,' began DI Todd.

'No!' protested Clive, 'I didn't kill her! She fell on the knife. It was a horrible accident.'

'How do you explain the strangulation marks on her neck? Marks which we have identified as being made by your hands?'

Clive's stomach ached and he felt nauseous. He swallowed hard.

'I admit, I did go for her. I was so angry – she was sitting on the bed, taunting me…'

'So you attempted to strangle her, but she fought back, ran to the kitchen and grabbed a knife to defend herself.'

'She ran downstairs and I followed her. But when I saw her holding the knife I tried to take it off her. We struggled, and she fell, onto the knife. As I said, it was a horrible accident.'

'We found your fingerprints on the knife.'

'Well, you would – I use it for cooking.'

DI Todd and his colleague exchanged a glance, then continued.

'When the ambulancemen arrived, they found you covered with your wife's blood.'

'I was distraught. I telephoned for help straightaway, then returned to Angela and I was holding her in my arms when the ambulance arrived. Of course I was covered with her blood!'

The DI paused to light a cigarette, offered one to Clive who declined, then said, 'we understand that you recently took out an insurance policy of two thousand pounds on your wife's life.'

'Yes, and my own life's insured for the same amount. That's my job, for heaven's sake, arranging insurance - it doesn't mean I'd kill her for it!'

DI Todd was unconvinced.

'It's still a tidy sum…'

'Angela's business was doing well. In fact, she was earning more than me, so it made sense for us both to be insured.'

Again, the detectives exchanged a look.

'Do you know the identity of your wife's lover?'

'No. A man pushed past me when I arrived home, but I didn't see who it was.'

'How long had her affair been going on?'

'I don't know.'

The DI finished his cigarette, stubbed it out in an ashtray then faced Clive.

'Mr Best, as I see it, you attacked a defenceless woman, and when she tried to fight back by grabbing a kitchen knife, you took the knife from her and stabbed her. You killed your wife, deliberately, in a jealous rage.'

'No! No! I've told you, it was an accident! I didn't murder Angela! I loved her!'

DI Todd sat back and looked at Clive, sceptically.

'I don't believe you. Clive Best, I am charging you with murder. Take him away.'

The story makes the front page of the Chronicle. 'Bath man charged with wife's murder' says the headline. But I don't believe he killed her deliberately. I saw the shock, the horror, in Mr Best's eyes when he was standing at the window, just after it happened - it was an accident, not murder. If only I could speak up for him: just because I can't communicate, it doesn't mean I have nothing to say.

Murder, being a capital offence, was outside the jurisdiction of the Bath courts and Clive was sent to Bristol prison to be held until his hearing at Bristol Crown Court. His barrister prepared his defence, going through the events of that fateful afternoon over and over again, but proving that Angela's death was accidental wasn't going to be easy. The barrister asked, 'are you absolutely sure there is nobody who witnessed what happened? A passer-by, or a neighbour, who may have seen something and could vouch for you?'

Clive recalled looking out the window as he stood over Angela's body, meeting the eyes of the disabled man in the house opposite. In that brief moment of connection he was sure the young man understood what had happened, and knew the truth. But what was the point of having a witness who couldn't speak?

So Clive shook his head and said, 'no one can help me.'

The trial commenced, with each day's proceedings reported by the *Chronicle* in lurid detail. Clive's barrister presented his case persuasively and summoned Clive's old boss and some of his colleagues to bear witness to his client's good character. The prosecutor, however, portrayed the accused as a man whose patience with his domineering wife had finally snapped in the face of her adultery, and unable to contain his resentment and anger, he had killed her. The Masons stayed out of the matter: there was some sympathy for Clive, but the brotherhood's chief concern was to protect the identity of Angela's lover, and they closed ranks.

As the evidence mounted, members of the jury found themselves being swayed by the prosecutor's arguments. After a two-week hearing the judge summed up and sent the jury to consider their verdict.

My father and Mrs Bird have been paying great attention to the reports of Clive Best's trial. Every evening she reads the latest to me from the Chronicle, savouring every detail. I am more convinced than ever that he is innocent, but I fear the worst.

The jury deliberated for five days then returned their verdict.

'GUILTY!'

Clive's legs buckled beneath him, and he had to be supported by the warders as the judge placed the black cap on his head and pronounced:

'Clive Arthur Best, you have been found guilty of murder. You will be taken hence to a lawful prison and from there to a place of execution where you will be hanged by the neck until dead. May the Lord have mercy upon your soul.'

I'm devastated to know that Mr Best has been found guilty of murder. I'm convinced he's been treated unjustly and am beyond frustration that I'm powerless to help him. I'll sit here for the rest of my life, wishing there was something I could have done to save his.

The fatal day arrived. At eight o'clock in the morning Clive was taken to the condemned cell where he was visited by a priest, then the hangman entered and bound the prisoner's hands behind his back with a leather strap. With a warder on either side of him, Clive, his heart racing and his whole body shaking, followed the hangman to the gallows room and was led into position, standing on the trapdoors. He broke into a cold sweat, still unable to understand how it had come to this. The hangman placed a white hood over Clive's head and positioned the noose around his neck while the assistants strapped his ankles.

For one last time, Clive cried out, 'it was an accident! I am innocent!'

But his words made no difference.

Everything was ready. The hangman pushed the lever to release the trapdoors and Clive plummeted into the void. The noose tightened, leaving him hanging motionless, his neck broken.

The last drop.

BRENDA'S BIG DATE

Brenda woke up and looked at the clock. Half past seven. Good, a nice early start. She was feeling excited, and tried to remember why. Yes, of course! This was her important day, the day she'd been looking forward to for so long…

Brenda got out of bed, put on her housecoat and went downstairs. She switched on the kettle, poured some cereal into a bowl and started to make plans. She was due to meet him at six o'clock for drinks, then he was going to take her to his favourite Italian restaurant for a meal. It must be years since she'd eaten Italian, she thought. Did they still have Chianti bottles wrapped in raffia on the tables, with candles in them, or were they out of fashion?

And thin breadsticks in a rustic pot? And oily black-haired waiters wielding those grotesque giant pepper grinders? She laughed at herself and her foolish memories. Well, it would be fun finding out.

She ate her breakfast at a leisurely pace and made herself a second cup of tea. No need to hurry today, she had plenty of time. She followed her usual routine, getting dressed and doing a few jobs around the house until the postman arrived at eleven o'clock. No letters, no bills, just catalogues advertising things she didn't want, but she enjoyed looking at the pictures while she drank her coffee.

She allowed herself a moment to daydream. What would he be like? The photo on the computer showed a handsome older gentleman – silver-haired, suntanned, smiling. He was called Gerald. She'd sent him lots of messages now, and he'd responded, so politely. When he finally suggested they should meet, she'd been completely overwhelmed. She put off replying for a long time, but finally plucked up the courage and said yes.

Brenda just had a slice of toast for lunch as she didn't want to spoil her appetite for this evening. She didn't cook for herself anymore – toast was all she could manage. She couldn't remember why, but they'd told her she mustn't use the oven, ever since that time when…

In any case she was beginning to feel a bit nervous, and wasn't very hungry.

In the afternoon she went up to her bedroom and opened her wardrobe. She had to decide what to wear for her big date.

'Date!' she said to herself, 'what a crazy, American word – I'm far too old to go on a date! But, whatever it's called, I'll have to wear something nice. Now, what do we have here…?'

She lost an hour, taking dress after dress out of her wardrobe and laying them on the bed. So many clothes, so many memories…

At last, she decided upon a navy blue, knee-length dress, understated but elegant. She tried it on to make sure it still fitted. Lord, she hadn't worn this since her husband was alive… Yes, it would be perfect.

The next hour passed in choosing suitable jewellery, and she even found an old bottle of perfume with a little left in the bottom. She'd forgotten what fun it was to dress up and go out for an evening. She wondered whether he – Gerald – was equally excited about meeting her tonight.

Nails next. The varnish was old and a bit clogged up but she managed to get enough out of the bottle for one coat. She had a cup of tea and a biscuit while the nail varnish dried. There were still lots of things she had to do. She would need to leave the house at half past five to get the bus into town for six o'clock. But she realised, in a panic, that it was already five o'clock. Where had the afternoon gone? She hadn't even washed up her plate from lunchtime yet. And this navy dress that she'd been wearing, it really could do with an iron before she went out in it.

She hadn't used the iron for a long time. She had a feeling she wasn't supposed to, but went ahead anyway. It took her a while to put up the ironing board, then she took off her dress, laid it on the board and arranged it in place. Standing in her petticoat, she began to manoeuvre the iron over the folds of her dress. For some reason she found it difficult to control, and in a moment of carelessness she caught the inside of her wrist on the hot plate. She cried out in shock, dropped the iron and went to the sink to run cold water over her burning wrist. As the pain began to ease she turned back and picked up the iron which had left a nasty brown scorch mark on the neckline of her dress.

'Stupid, stupid, stupid!' she cussed herself. She would just have to go upstairs and choose something else to wear. But it was half past five - she'd missed the bus. Never mind, there'd be another one in half an hour, she'd just be a bit late, that's all…

At six o'clock the front doorbell rang.

Brenda went to answer it, still in her underwear.

'Hello Brenda,' said a friendly voice, then looking her up and down, she added, 'you haven't been ironing again, have you? Oh, you are naughty, Brenda, you know you should leave that to me!'

Brenda looked sheepish and the woman, who was dressed in her uniform of a light-blue tunic and matching trousers, entered the hallway.

'I know, Sheila, but I wanted to wear my navy dress. I'm going out tonight, to meet Gerald.'

'Of course you are,' said Sheila.

'Well, I *was* going to…but it got so late, what with deciding what to wear, and the iron and all that…and I've missed the bus now…'

Brenda began to cry.

'Don't worry, darling,' said Sheila, putting her arm around Brenda's shoulders to comfort her, 'I'm sure Gerald will be able to meet you another time. Now, let's get you dressed, then you can sit down while I make your tea. I've got lasagne for you tonight!'

Brenda sat down, obediently.

'Thank you, Sheila. That will be nice. I like Italian food.'

*

The following morning, Brenda woke up and looked at the clock. Half past seven. Good, a nice early start. She was feeling excited, and tried to remember why. Yes, of course! This was her important day, the day she'd been looking forward to for so long…

GOAT RODEO

'I thought I'd organise a birthday party for your Dad,' said Kate Henderson, speaking on her mobile to her daughter, Emily.

'But Dad hates parties!'

'I know, but I can't let his sixtieth go unmarked – and when I say '*party*', what I really mean is, just a few drinks with the family, and the neighbours, and a couple of his friends… Hopefully the weather will still be good, and we can hold it in the garden.'

'Hmmm – you will tell him, though? He doesn't like surprises…'

'Yes, of course I will. I'm sure I can persuade him.'

'I suppose you'll want us to help?'

'Please – I'll make out a list and see who can do what.'

'Well good luck with that…'

Jeremy Henderson wasn't enthusiastic.

'Do we have to? Can't we just go out for a quiet dinner for two?'

'But your sixtieth is special!' said Kate. 'You're retiring – it's an important milestone. And we all want to have the chance to celebrate with you.'

'Do we?'

'Yes! Oh, go on – you'll enjoy it when it comes, and you don't have to do a thing – I'll organise it all.'

'That's what I'm afraid of…'

The following day at his dental practice, Jeremy told his assistant what his wife was planning.

'Awesome!' she responded, 'the end of your career – it's an occasion worth marking. How long have you been in dentistry?'

'It will be thirty-five years since I qualified.'

'Wow! Before I was born!'

'Thanks, Poppy – that makes me feel better…'

The next weekend Emily came to her parents' home, a pleasant, detached house in suburban Surrey, with her husband, Suraj, and baby daughter, Amber. The Summer of 2022 had seen some of the highest temperatures ever recorded in England, but this particular August day was more moderate, giving the family a chance to relax in the garden in the shade of a parasol with some Pimms, the baby contentedly in her carrycot on a rug.

'So, Mum, you've got a month to organise Dad's party – not long!'

'There's plenty of time. And as I said, it will only be a small affair. His birthday's on a Sunday so I thought we'd start at lunchtime and people can stay into the afternoon.'

'It will be nice to have a get-together – it will be the first party we've been to since Amber was born.'

'And for us it's the first since the Covid lockdown ended. It's a good excuse to entertain again.'

'Are you going to send out invitations?'

'I suppose I should…I'll do it tomorrow.'

When Kate got round to writing out the guest list she found it was longer than she'd anticipated, but on the basis that some people wouldn't be able to make it she went ahead and sent out fifty invitations. Then, sitting down with her morning coffee, she started her list of things to do.

That evening after dinner, Jeremy was reading his newspaper when he suddenly exclaimed, 'Good God! This is terrible!'

'What is it, darling?'

'It's the Red Arrows – awful goings-on!'

He read out an extract from that day's 'Telegraph':

'No wonder the Red Arrows are in a spin: 'Boozy training exercises', alleged adultery and 'toxic' culture revealed after three of the elite squadron quit or were suspended.'

'I don't believe it!'

Being a big fan of the Red Arrows and all things aviation, Jeremy took this news to heart. He and the family had spent many happy weekends visiting Air Shows which frequently concluded with a heart-stopping performance from the famous display team. Learning that his heroes had feet of clay made him feel let-down, disillusioned, even at his age.

'There's more!' he continued.

'…claims of bullying and sexual harassment…allegations of misogyny, assault and drunkenness reportedly made as more than forty personnel testify in internal investigation.'

'What on earth's been going on?' asked Kate, looking at the article over her husband's shoulder.

'God knows. It looks as if their training periods in Greece involved more than just manoeuvres in the sky…They're down to performing with only seven planes, apparently, and it says here they might even be disbanded altogether!'

'That would be awful!'

'There's going to be a full investigation into the Squadron's behaviour. Hopefully the inquiry will root-out the bad apples and sort it out. God knows what my father will make of all this!'

Jeremy's father, Howard Henderson, had spent his wartime boyhood in awe of the brave pilots who fought the Battle of Britain, and the day he signed up for his National Service with the RAF in 1950 was his dream come true. He'd gone on to have a distinguished career, retiring as a Wing Commander, and although he'd had a lucrative second career in industry, his time in the RAF was closest to his heart. He'd passed his love of aviation to his son, but due to colour-blindness Jeremy was unable to join as a pilot, a disappointment for them both.

Jeremy's life had taken an altogether different turn, studying for a science degree and falling head over heels in love with Kate, one of his fellow students. He'd followed her into dentistry and together they'd built up a successful practice, which she had left some years earlier to raise their three children. But Jeremy retained his interest in anything flying-related, and as the Red Arrows display team was his particular favourite, he felt the distress at their predicament almost personally.

The next weekend Jeremy was discussing the matter with his friends at the local golf club when a visiting American joined in their discussion.

'What a mess!' he declared, as more tales of boorish behaviour, heavy drinking and inappropriate sex emerged, then he added, 'a real Goat Rodeo!'

'What do you mean?' asked Jeremy.

'At home it's what aviators call a massive cock-up, when everything that can go wrong, does go wrong - a situation totally out of control. Sounds like you've got one of those with your Red Arrows, for sure.'

The Red Arrows' problems faded from the headlines and Jeremy concentrated on the last weeks of his career. He was selling the dental practice to a younger colleague, accepting that his time was up, and retirement beckoned.

'What are you going to do?' asked Poppy, his assistant.

Jeremy sighed. It was a big change which he still wasn't sure how to manage.

'I'll play golf more often,' he began, 'and Kate has a long list of jobs she wants me to do at home… Then there's the children, of course, and the grandchildren, but I've warned them, I'm not going to become a permanent babysitter.'

'Quite right! You've worked all this time, and now it's your turn to have some fun.'

'Exactly! Kate wants to travel, so we'll do some of that. And I want to go to our local airfield, get involved, see if there's anything I can do. I won't be able to fly, but I'm sure there's a place for an enthusiast.'

'Sounds great! Better than doing Mr Dickinson's root canal treatment - which awaits us now…!'

At home, Kate was progressing with the arrangements for Jeremy's party.

'So I've asked the caterers to provide a buffet for up to fifty people, something up-market – not dreary little sausage rolls on plastic plates. They prepare everything in advance in their kitchen, bring it here and they supply crockery, cutlery and glasses.'

'Who are you using?' asked Emily.

'A new company called Parties Are Us, in the High Street. The woman there seems reliable.'

'Good. You can borrow our gazebo – I'll get Suraj to put it up.'

'Thank you. And you can bring some picnic chairs. I've asked Adam to make a cake.'

Adam, Kate and Jeremy's elder son, lived in London with his partner Annabel and two children. They lived what Kate considered to be an unconventional lifestyle, with financier Annabel working in the City while Adam stayed at home, doing the odd bit of freelance writing and looking after his increasingly wayward children. He assured his mother that his domestic arrangements were quite normal among his circle, and there were benefits, such as his newly-discovered baking skills.

'And what about Nathan…?'

Relations with Nathan, the younger son, had been difficult ever since that awful night when he'd stormed out after a terrible row with his father. The two hadn't spoken for over a year.

'Yes…I've invited him, but whether he'll come, I don't know. Do you think you could work on him?'

'I'll try,' said Emily.

Jeremy paid a visit to his father, aged ninety, who lived alone in what was termed a 'luxury retirement village' close by. Fiercely independent, he had looked after himself since his wife had died some thirty years before. In spite of his advancing years he retained his military bearing and perfectly groomed moustache along with a positive outlook on life. He made Jeremy feel quite inadequate.

'I've received an invitation to your birthday party!' he said.

'Good! Although I hadn't realised it was that formal – just family and a few friends, Kate told me…'

'You should know your wife better than that by now! Anyway, I will be pleased to attend. There can't be many fathers who are still around to celebrate their son's retirement. I'll ask one of the staff here to drive me over.'

Jeremy made some coffee in the espresso machine and they sat down in the well-equipped kitchen. Jeremy looked into his cup and sighed.

'What's the matter?' asked Howard.

'Sorry! I didn't mean to sound miserable! It's just this birthday, I suppose, and retiring – makes me feel old!'

'As my military colleagues used to say - it depends which end of the telescope you're looking through. I mean, from my perspective you're still a young man!'

'Of course…but it doesn't feel like that to me!'

'You need to look upon retirement as a fresh start, like a new career – it's a beginning, not an end. Think of all the things you've been wanting to do and grab the chance to do them while you can. You and Kate are all right, aren't you? And the children?'

'Yes…yes, I'm very lucky.'

He didn't mention the argument with Nathan which he still found difficult to confront.

'And your health is good?'

'It is, thank God, although, I have been thinking… I'm coming up to the same age as Mum was when she died.'

Howard's face clouded for a moment. Those years when his wife was suffering from cancer were the worst of his life and he didn't like to dwell on them.

'Certainly… but there's no reason to think that you'll go down that route. One must stay positive, Jeremy – it's the only way to get through life. It doesn't get any easier, you know, one just has to stick at it.'

Jeremy nodded at the words of his wise old father. They were silent for a moment, then to change the direction of the conversation

Jeremy asked, 'did you read about the Red Arrows in the newspaper?'

'Yes! What is the RAF coming to? Wouldn't have happened in my day!'

'Sometimes I despair of the modern world. I mean, what were they thinking?'

'This inquiry they're holding should sort it out. The RAF won't let the Red Arrows fail – they're too important for PR.'

'Good point. I hope you're right, Dad.'

The end of September approached, and with it, Jeremy's final day at the practice. He saw his last patient, cleaned up and said to Poppy, 'so that's it – my last ever filling!'

'I'm pleased for you! We'll miss you, though.'

'I don't think my patients will…'

Jeremy had learnt early in his career that nobody loves the dentist. However pleasant and professional one tried to be, nobody came for pleasure, and even when one had put a patient out of the misery of toothache there was rarely any show of gratitude. 'I spend hours using all my skills to treat people's pain, create crowns and fillings that will last for years, and all they do is moan about how much it costs! It really is the most undervalued profession,' he would say, resentfully, to friends at dinner parties.

'At least your colleagues appreciate you,' said Poppy.

'Mmm – where are they all, anyway?'

'Everyone's busy.'

'Right…well I'll toddle off then. Goodbye, Poppy, and thank you.'

As he reached the door, she added, 'see you on Sunday!'

He turned, surprised.

'At your party! Your wife's invited us all!'

'Has she indeed…'

He left the room and closed the door, a small smile on his lips.

On Saturday, Emily and Suraj brought over the gazebo and put it up with Jeremy's help. As they worked, Suraj asked, 'so, how's retirement?'

'It's my first day, give me a chance! Ask me in a few months. But with this party and the other things Kate's got lined up for me I don't think I'll be bored…'

Emily helped her mother set out some picnic tables and chairs, preparing as much as they could in advance knowing that the next day would be busy, with guests expected from midday. With fairy lights and bunting it all looked very festive. Kate stood back, admiring their efforts, and took Jeremy's arm in hers.

'You see, darling? It's going to be lovely. A proper celebration for your birthday!'

That evening, Jeremy closed the patio doors and sniffed the air. The weather had turned cooler with a distinct breeze.

'I hope there's not going to be a storm,' he said.

'No, I looked at the forecast and there's nothing predicted,' said Kate.

At three o'clock they were woken by a ferocious wind blowing and rain lashing against the window.

'What the…? I thought you said the forecast was good!'

'It was!'

'You can't trust the Met Office!'

Together, they looked out the bedroom window. Rain was pouring down the street and the trees were blown horizontal.

'It's dreadful out there!'

'I know! But there's nothing we can do now. Let's go back to bed and we'll see how things look in the morning.'

At eight o'clock, Kate and Jeremy went downstairs to find a scene of devastation. A large branch had fallen from a tree bordering the lawn, demolishing the gazebo, leaving a soggy wreck and pieces of canvas strewn around the garden. The bunting and lights had gone, the plastic chairs were blown all over the shop, one of the panes in the greenhouse had smashed and the fence at the bottom of the garden was wrecked.

'It's awful!' cried Kate, 'everything's ruined!'

At that moment her phone rang.

'Mrs Henderson? It's the caterer from 'Parties Are Us.' I'm afraid that after the storm last night our kitchen's flooded and we can't work. I'm so sorry but we won't be able to do the food for your party.'

Kate's heart sank. She told Jeremy the news.

'It's a disaster!' she wailed, 'we'll have to cancel.'

She looked so disappointed that Jeremy felt sorry for her, knowing how much effort she'd put into organising everything. Although he hadn't been keen on the idea at first, by now he was quite looking forward to his party and it seemed a shame to let it go.

'Don't give up yet,' he said. 'The storm's blown through and it looks like it's going to be a nice day. Let's sit down and work out what we can do.'

Kate looked at him in surprise.

'All right…'

'We can't let this party turn into a Goat Rodeo!'

After some thought and several cups of coffee they made a plan to rescue the birthday celebrations. Kate rang her daughter and explained the situation.

'We need an emergency run to Waitrose! I'll come and pick you up. And please send Suraj over here to help your father sort out the garden.'

Suraj arrived with his chainsaw and cleared the large branch from the lawn. Together he and Jeremy collected up the remnants of the gazebo and started to erect another one that Suraj had borrowed from a friend. Then Kate and Emily returned, looking despondent.

'It's hopeless,' said Kate, 'the Fire Brigade have closed several streets due to flooding and the shops are shut. We can't buy any food!'

'At least we've got plenty of champagne!' said Jeremy.

'But we're going to need something to eat! I can't feed fifty people from what I've got in the freezer.'

'Fifty?!'

'Well, I didn't expect everyone I invited to accept!'

'That is quite a crowd…no wonder you were hoping for a fine day so we could use the garden. Now, there must be something we can do.'

Jeremy thought for a moment, then declared, 'hang on…I've got an idea.'

He went to make a call and returned with a broad smile.

'All fixed!'

Kate and Emily were astonished.

'I had a word with Doreen, the catering manager at the golf club. They escaped the worst of the storm over there and are still functioning. She's promised to rustle up a buffet and bring it over later.'

'That's amazing! How did you persuade her to do that?'

'Well… do you remember that time her false teeth broke and I gave her an emergency repair?'

'Yes, I do… she had a dinner dance that night and was worried she'd have to miss it!'

'She was very grateful, and hadn't forgotten. She said she owed me one!'

At eleven o'clock Adam, the elder son, arrived from London with his partner and children in tow. They got out the car, Annabel shouting at the children to 'stop looking at that phone and go and say hello to your grandparents!' Sky, aged ten, and her brother River, aged eight, went to their Grandma who hugged them, then to Grandad who ruffled their hair and told them they'd grown.

'We had a terrible storm last night,' said Kate, 'I'm pleased you've arrived early, you can help us with the clearing up.'

Adam took a large tupperware box from the car and carried it carefully into the kitchen.

'The cake! Can I see?'

'No - it's a surprise!'

Everyone went into the garden, the adults arranging a new set of borrowed chairs and tables while Sky cooed over baby Amber, and River curled up on the damp grass.

'Is he all right?' asked Kate.

'Yes,' replied Sky, 'he says it's his natural position. He's self-identifying as a cat this week.'

Emily had a quiet word with her mother.

'I'm going to fetch Nathan, I've persuaded him to come. I had to do the big-sister thing but he got the message.'

'Thank you, Emily, well done! I hope your father takes it the right way. I'll try and prepare him.'

Kate popped upstairs to get dressed and came down in a jazzy pair of palazzo pants and a white top. With make-up applied and hair brushed she felt ready to face the world and whatever the rest of the day threw at her. She joined her husband in the garden just as the next-door neighbours appeared, carrying more chairs, drinks and bunting.

'You've done a grand job,' said one of them. 'After that dreadful storm last night we wondered whether you'd still go ahead.'

'It was a shame not to,' replied Jeremy. 'I'm pleased you could come, and thanks for the extra bits and pieces.'

'The least we can do, after everything you've done for us over the years. Remember that weekend you sorted out my raging toothache? – absolute life-saver!'

At midday Jeremy's father arrived to a warm welcome, smart as ever in a Panama hat, collar and tie, leaning on his walking stick with an air of confidence, enjoying the attention that came with being the senior family member. He was the only person the children were in awe of, and even River stopped being a cat for a moment as he and his sister went to say hello to their Great-Grandad and escorted him as he slowly made his way into the garden.

The sun had come out, champagne corks were popping and other guests flooded in, including Jeremy's colleagues from the practice who apologised for not giving him a proper send-off from work, and promising to make it up to him today. Then Doreen arrived from the golf club with trays of food which a grateful Kate helped to set out in the kitchen.

'I can't thank you enough!' she said, 'you must stay and join us!'

'I would, but I've got to get back. Just give me a ring if you need anything else. Your husband rescued me once and I'm happy to repay the compliment!'

Some of Jeremy's colleagues had brought their young children with them, hoping they would behave themselves. At first, a younger boy joined River on the ground to play cats with him until River objected, explaining that he was a *real* cat, at which point the other child lost interest. Meanwhile his sister Sky was busy taking selfies, practising poses to share with her sophisticated London friends, and bonding with an older girl over their shared love of an influencer on TikTok. Unfortunately, two of the boys who had taken an instant dislike to each other came to blows over nothing at all and parents had to intervene, one of the dentists memorably threatening his son by hissing, 'behave, or I'll take all your teeth out!'

Jeremy was beginning to relax and enjoy himself after the earlier traumas of the day, when Kate took him to one side.

'Emily's gone to fetch a special guest.'

He raised his eyebrows.

'It's Nathan.'

His face darkened.

'Please don't get angry! I couldn't bear to think of him not being here with us all. I know it's difficult between you, but please try. He wants to see you.'

'Have you seen him?'

'A couple of times, yes.'

'You didn't tell me.'

'Well, I knew you wouldn't like it. Look, they'll be here soon, so please be civil. And nowadays it's no big deal…'

They heard a car outside and Emily came in accompanied by a striking blonde, dressed in a slinky crimson number and matching heels. He looked at Jeremy, hesitated, then said, 'happy birthday, Dad.'

Emily stood holding Nathan's arm, providing moral support, while Jeremy stared at him. Nathan stepped forward and presented his father with a gift bag.

'It's a decent bottle of Bordeaux, I hope you like it.'

Jeremy couldn't bring himself to speak. He looked at the person in front of him, trying to see signs of the boy he knew and loved under the make-up and fancy clothes.

'I'm sorry we argued, Dad, but I couldn't see any way out back then. I've spent a year finding myself – and this is who I am.'

Kate went and put her arm around him.

'Welcome back, Nathan. We've missed you.'

'Thanks, Mum. I've missed you too. I call myself 'Natalie' now, if you don't mind. And my pronouns are female.'

'Of course. All right, Natalie,' Kate said, and kissed her on the cheek.

Standing between her mother and sister, her confidence growing, Natalie smiled, revealing a set of perfect teeth. Jeremy suddenly remembered his son at twelve, his mouth a tangle of wires devised to straighten his uneven teeth. Well, at least that had worked – but what about the rest of him?

Maybe it was the effect of too much champagne, but in spite of himself Jeremy felt a softening of his attitude, of the need to live and let live. He knew such things happened; he just hadn't expected it in his own family. But Nathan was an adult, he could do what he wanted, and it could be worse. There would be gossip at the golf club but that was too bad. Forever formal, Jeremy put out his right hand, Natalie responded and shook it.

'All right… er… Natalie...bear with me, won't you – it will take me a while to get used to this. But if you're happy, that's all I can ask.'

That smile again.

'Thanks, Dad – yes, I am.'

'Right – you'd better come and join the party!'

The weather was bright and breezy, the food was going down well, and Jeremy looked around at the assembled guests, impressed – he hadn't realised he had so many friends. Natalie was chatting to Poppy, Emily was in a discreet corner feeding her baby, Adam and Annabel looked happy and relaxed together, away from the pressures of the city, and Kate was circulating among the guests, the consummate hostess, flourishing in the social scene which he always found such a trial. He wandered over and stood next to his father who was seated in a sturdy chair in the shade.

'I'm pleased it's worked out for you, Jeremy – I was a bit worried last night, with that storm.'

'Yes – we managed to retrieve the situation, with help from a lot of people.'

'You've done well – it's a fine way to mark your birthday and a successful career. I'm proud of you.'

Surprised at the unaccustomed praise, Jeremy said, 'thanks, Dad!', then to steer the conversation away from becoming sentimental, added, 'by the way, did you read the latest about the Red Arrows? Looks like they've sacked some staff and are putting the whole team through training to improve behaviour and culture.'

'Let's hope that sorts them out.'

'Yes – it would have been a tragedy to lose them.'

Looking around at the guests, Howard said, 'tell me, who's that rather attractive blonde over there?'

'Don't be shocked, but that is your grandson, Nathan – who wants to be known as Natalie.'

'Really?!'

'It's what seems to happen nowadays…'

'Oh, I don't know – when I was in the RAF we often used to dress up as women…you know, for entertainment purposes…I say, she's got rather good legs – reminds me of my dear wife!'

It was time to present the cake, so Adam went to the kitchen and carried it carefully into the garden. The large, semi-circular sponge cake was covered in pink icing with two rows of rounded white rectangles along the curved edge, designed to look like a set of teeth. In the centre was a sugar paste model of a dentist in his whites, holding a probe and a mirror, and two lit candles in the shape of a six and a nought.

The crowd clapped with delight.

Jeremy was touched.

'It's magnificent!' he cried, 'I can't bear to cut it!'

'At least blow out the candles!' said Kate.

He did so, everyone sang 'Happy Birthday' and Jeremy beamed as people got out their phones to take his picture. He looked at the crowd, seeing so many people he knew and loved, feeling their warmth and appreciation, then put his arm around Kate's shoulders and gave her a kiss. In that golden moment the kids stopped squabbling, the baby didn't cry, Adam, Emily and Natalie were standing together, siblings united, Sky was chatting happily to her Great-Grandad, River was curled up on the ground, purring, the breeze dropped and the sun shone.

Not a goat in sight.

Suddenly, just as it seemed things couldn't get any better, there was a mighty roar above their heads and everyone looked skywards, watching in awe as nine Red Arrows flew directly overhead, the sun glinting on them, brilliant against the bluest of skies, in perfect formation.

A VILLAGE CALLED 'PERFECT'

'Oh, come on, Beth – it's my birthday!' said Vicky.

I didn't really want to go to the pub; it was an unexpectedly warm Saturday evening at the end of September, we'd been serving customers at the café non-stop all day and I was keen to get back to my flat, strip off and sit in the garden with a long, cool drink. But Vicky was persistent.

'Please - just stay for a quick one!'

Arm twisted, I left the café with Andy the cook, and waitresses Lyn and Hayley. Vicky, the owner, locked the door and led us up the road to a pub on Lansdown Hill. A native of Bath, I'd worked for Vicky off and on for three years at her place in the Abbey Churchyard, starting as a washer-upper when still at school, then taking a permanent job as a waitress and baker, having discovered a talent for making pastries. I'd been on my feet all day – it had been a busy one, given the good weather, and I really wanted some peace and quiet, but Vicky was a friend as well as the boss so I thought I'd better be sociable, for a little while at least. We reached the Lansdown Arms which was cool but gloomy, so while the birthday girl ordered our drinks the rest of us went outside to sit in the beer garden.

Vicky arrived with drinks on a tray and we all gave her a toast. Her plan was to have a few here before moving on to another pub, then go for a Chinese. After a couple of rounds I was thinking of an excuse to get away when Vicky touched my arm and said, 'see that lad over there? He keeps staring at you!'

I glanced over to another table where two young men were sitting, drinking pints of cider. The one with dark hair was talking, and although the fair-haired one was pretending to listen, he was definitely looking in my direction.

'Do you know him?'

'I don't think so.'

'He's nice-looking, isn't he?'

'Yes – he is rather.'

'We ought to invite them over.'

'No!'

'Beth, you'll never meet anyone if you go on like that!'

I knew my lack of a boyfriend was a standing joke among my colleagues and a source of speculation, but the truth was I just hadn't met the right person yet. I was a bit overweight - all those pastries - and felt self-conscious about my ginger hair and freckles, so had low expectations on the romantic front. It came as a surprise to have sparked someone's interest and I didn't think a handsome fellow like this would give me a second look, but I must have had something because he came over to speak to us.

'Can I buy you lovely ladies a drink on this warm evening?'

He spoke with a gentle Somerset burr, had the most fetching smile and sky-blue eyes. I was sure we hadn't met before, and yet – something about the cut of his jawline, his ruddy cheeks, seemed familiar.

We ordered two halves of cider and both lads joined us.

He introduced himself as Simon, and his dark-haired friend was Will, who was a bit young for Vicky, but she looked on with wry amusement as Simon chatted me up. At twenty, he was two years older than me, his hair was cut short (unusual for the time, this being the seventies) and he wore a loose, collarless shirt. For my part I was in a cheesecloth top tied around my midriff and bell-bottomed jeans, nothing special. But for all of it, he seemed attracted to me, asking about myself and quickly establishing that I didn't have a boyfriend, and I felt drawn to him, too. After an hour or so his friend had to leave, and Vicky and the others were ready to move on.

'You're welcome to come if you want,' said Vicky, to both of us.

I hesitated for a moment.

'No, it's OK, I'll just stay here for a bit longer, then go home.'

'Thanks for asking,' said Simon, 'but I think I'll stay too – if that's all right?' he asked, looking at me.

'Of course!'

As she left, Vicky gave me a smile and squeezed my shoulder.

I would never see her again.

*

Left alone, Simon and I found ourselves absorbed in conversation. He told me he worked on his parents' cider farm in a little village near Glastonbury and had come to Bath to discuss business with his friend, Will, who ran an off-licence. Before I knew it the evening had flown, the barman called time and Simon leaned towards me, saying, 'I'm staying in Bath for the weekend. I've got some business to attend to in the morning, but would you like to meet me tomorrow afternoon?'

I looked into his lovely blue eyes and said, 'yes, I'd like that.'

We parted and I walked back to my flat on a cloud. I spent all night thinking about the handsome stranger, still wondering why he had homed-in on me and with a strong feeling that there was some kind of connection between us. I opened the diary I kept on my bedside table but my mind was so overwhelmed I couldn't even write a sentence to describe how I felt, just managing to jot down a few words before finally falling asleep.

The next morning dragged, I was so excited about seeing Simon again. Normally I spend Sundays cleaning the flat and doing my washing but that day I couldn't concentrate on the simplest of tasks. The weather was still warm and I wanted to wear something cool and loose, so settled on my favourite Laura Ashley dress, a floaty style in a floral pattern with a low neckline, showing my best assets. We'd agreed to meet at the balustrade overlooking the Parade Gardens, and as I approached I saw him there, watching the boats on the river.

He turned and when he saw me a smile lit up his face.

'Beth, you look beautiful!'

No one had ever told me that before. I blushed, we laughed and he gave me a kiss on the cheek, his closeness making my heart go all a-flutter.

We spent the afternoon walking around Bath enjoying the sights on this sunny Sunday afternoon, me seeing my home city in a whole new light. At seven he took me to a restaurant where we talked and talked like old friends, both of us feeling that we'd known each other for years. Then he asked, 'are you doing anything tomorrow?'

'No - the café's closed on Mondays. Why?'

'I'd like to take you to see my village and meet my family.'

I laughed. 'It's a bit soon for all that, isn't it?'

He turned serious.

'No,' he said, 'I don't think it is.'

He took my hands in his and said, 'Beth, I knew as soon as I saw you that you were the girl for me. Let's not waste any time! I want to have you in my life, and I don't want to wait!'

I was shocked. Could I trust this man whom I'd met only yesterday?

He let me go and sat back in his chair.

'I'm sorry, Beth, I'm getting carried away. I mustn't rush you! Although… I was hoping you might feel the same way. I was awake all last night, thinking about you!'

'Me too!'

He smiled, a warm, loving smile, and took my hands again.

'Look – would you like to spend the day with me tomorrow? I could pick you up at ten, we'll be in my village by midday, Mum will cook us lunch and I'll have you back home by evening. How does that sound?'

We locked eyes again.

'It sounds wonderful,' I said.

He picked me up at ten, as promised. I wore another floral number, feeling feminine and pretty for the first time in my life, and saw the appreciation in his eyes. I got in the car beside him and he steered out of Bath, heading south towards Glastonbury and the Somerset Levels. There wasn't a radio in his car and I fell into my habit of humming a song, something which I knew drove my colleagues at the café mad. Simon seemed to enjoy it, though, encouraging me through my repertoire of tunes ancient and modern, even joining in with some old folk songs my mother had taught me.

'You sing beautifully!' he said, 'you make the songs come alive. I don't know how you remember all those words!'

'Oh, I learnt them by heart when I was a child, so it's easy to remember.'

I launched into my favourite, *'Barbara Allen'*, and as I reached the end of the tragic tale we decided to stop for a break. He pulled off the main road, parked in a country lane, and I sat down on a patch of grass while he rummaged in the boot of the car, emerging with two glasses of cider.

'Makes a change from morning coffee!' I said, enjoying the cool, refreshing drink which had a distinctive flavour.

'One of our best brews!' he said as we clinked glasses.

We got back in the car and resumed our drive. It must have been the cider, but I felt sleepy and couldn't keep my eyes open. When I apologised he smiled and said, 'it's all right, have a snooze and I'll wake you up when we get there.'

I don't know how much time passed, but when I awoke I was sitting on a wooden bench, next to him. I looked around, confused. There was no sign of the car.

'Where am I?'

'You were in such a deep sleep I didn't want to wake you. They don't allow cars in the village, so I parked just outside and carried you here.'

My surroundings slowly came into focus. We were sitting on a village green next to a duck pond, bordering a street of traditional, stone-built houses. An elderly couple walked by and wished us good day, and a horse pulling a cart clopped along the road.

'It's lovely!' I said, slowly taking in the tranquil scene, 'what a gorgeous place.'

'Well, I did tell you!'

'Of course – when you said you came from a village called Perfect I didn't believe you! I can understand now, though.'

He gestured into the distance. 'My parents live just over there, on the farm. Come on, let's go!'

He got up and pulled me to my feet. We walked hand in hand, up the road and along a lane, passing rows and rows of apple trees.

'This is one of our orchards. We've almost finished the apple harvest – it's our busiest time of year. There's just a few remaining now.'

At the end of the lane we reached the farmhouse, an ancient dwelling with a thatched roof. We were met by Simon's mother, a lady in her forties with a round, kind face, her greying hair pulled back into a bun. She was wearing a long skirt with a starched apron around her waist and welcomed me warmly, as if she'd been expecting me.

'And you're…?'

'Beth,' said Simon.

She beamed at me and we shook hands, then Simon's father entered the room.

'This is Beth,' said his mother, already looking at me with fondness.

'Very pleased to meet you!' his father said, taking my hand and shaking it with a firm grip.

'And you, Mr…'

I realised I didn't even know Simon's surname.

'Fairfax, but you can call me Tom. And my wife is Marjorie.'

They stood, looking at me with curiosity, then Marjorie said, 'you must be hungry after your journey. Come through to the kitchen and we'll have something to eat.'

The country-style kitchen was charmingly old-fashioned, with a huge open fireplace. We sat at a long, wooden table, very rustic, and I admired the bunches of dried flowers and herbs hanging from the ceiling, filling the room with their pungent scent.

'What a lovely house!' I said, admiringly, 'so authentic!'

The three of them smiled at me.

'I knew you'd like it,' said Simon.

Marjorie served up platefuls of roast pork with fresh vegetables from the garden, a delicious feast washed down with cider, naturally. I tried hard to stay awake this time, and in response to their questions I told them about my life in Bath and my family – not that there was much to tell.

'My mother died when I was nine and I was brought up by my father,' I explained. 'There was just the two of us, then Dad re-married. My step-mother was keen to move back to her home in Yorkshire and persuaded Dad to go with her.'

'You live on your own, then?' asked Marjorie.

'Yes. I wanted to stay in Bath, and Dad bought me my flat. I see him occasionally. I still miss my mother – she was a gentle soul.'

'On the way here Beth was singing some old folk songs her mother taught her – she has a lovely voice!' said Simon, turning to me.

'Thank you! In fact, Mum came from round this way, from Langport. She used to fill me with tales of the old days, and our ancestors who fought in the Civil War.'

'Really? And whose side were they on?'

'Cromwell's, of course!'

There was a visible sigh of relief.

With a grin, Simon said, 'see, I knew she was the girl for me!'

I needed the bathroom and Simon escorted me to the back of the house.

'I'm afraid it's a bit basic. We're waiting to get some work done.'

He showed me outside to a wooden shed with a hole in the ground and a pail of water. I was shocked at first, then said, 'I suppose it's no worse than camping!'

After lunch Simon showed me around the village, so quaint, with small old-fashioned shops, horses trotting by pulling carts, and friendly people in vintage clothing.

'It reminds me of those open-air museums you can visit, you know, where it's like it was in the old days.'

'Yes, I know what you mean. Just one difference – this is real!'

I laughed at his joke, then my attention was caught by a distinguished-looking man riding by on a black stallion, acknowledging people with a nod of his head. The men lifted their hats as he passed and the women dipped in a small curtsey.

'Who's he?' I asked.

'That's Squire Marlow, the head of the village. Nothing happens here without him knowing about it.'

A chill breeze suddenly blew and Simon looked up at the leaden sky with concern.

'We'd better get back – looks as if there's going to be a storm.'

His prediction was correct. We'd only just returned to the farmhouse when the heavens opened and a mighty clap of thunder blasted overhead. It grew dark and Marjorie lit some candles while we sat in the warmth of the fire, pleased to be safely indoors while rain hammered down. After an hour the raging storm showed no sign of abating.

'I'm sorry, Beth, but I won't be able to get you back home tonight, not in these conditions,' said Simon. 'The roads around here will turn to mud.'

I looked out at water surging down the street, knowing the area was prone to flooding.

'You're welcome to stay, my dear,' said Marjorie, 'I can make up the spare bed for you, it's no trouble.'

There was no choice, but I didn't mind – Simon's family were so kind and hospitable, and I was enjoying my stay in this most unusual place.

'Thank you – that would be great.'

Later Simon showed me to my room, guiding me by candlelight, and left a candle burning in my room. He made up the wood fire, then, aware of his parents just downstairs, gave me a chaste kiss on the cheek and bade me goodnight.

I slept well and awoke in the morning to find that the storm had passed, but the road outside had turned into a river, awash with branches and debris. I put on the dress I'd worn yesterday and went downstairs where the others were up and about.

The first thing Simon said to me was, 'I'm sorry, Beth, it's too dangerous to venture out - the roads are impassable. This is the worst I've seen it in years. I'm afraid you'll have to stay here a little longer than planned.'

'It's all right – I don't mind,' I said, worried by the floods but excited at the prospect of spending more time with the Fairfax's.

'I'll need to ring the café though, to let them know I'm OK.'

'Sorry, you won't be able to, the phone lines are down because of the storm.'

'Oh - all right. I'll get in touch as soon as I can.'

*

On Tuesday morning Vicky opened the café and asked the others, 'do you know where Beth is? It's not like her to be late.'

'No, I haven't seen her since Saturday,' said Andy the cook.

'Nor me,' said Lyn and Hayley.

'I left her in the Lansdown Arms with that chap, Simon… I hope she's all right!'

'Probably overslept…' said Andy with a smirk.

The thunderstorm the night before had cleared the air and the café was busy with customers. Vicky was rushed off her feet, being one member of staff down, and it was only later that she thought, I hope Beth's okay – I expect she'll turn up tomorrow.

∗

The next day the flood water receded, leaving a deluge of mud. Simon went out to check for damage and returned, exhausted, saying, 'I reached the orchard but the rain's ruined much of the remaining crop. Thank goodness we'd already gathered most of it. There's a lot of clearing up to do.'

'I could stay and help!' I declared.

'Thank you, that would be wonderful!'

∗

When Beth didn't come to work on Wednesday, Vicky grew concerned. She telephoned her at home but there was no answer, then found a number for Beth's father who said he hadn't seen or heard from his daughter. After closing the café that evening Vicky went round to Beth's basement flat, rang the doorbell and peered through the window but there was no sign of anyone at home. With a growing feeling of foreboding, she decided to report the matter to the police.

'Do you think she might be with this Simon fellow?' the officer asked.

'Perhaps… she was with him when I last saw her.'

'And where might they have gone?'

'I don't know! He said he came from a small village in Somerset – perhaps he took her there.'

'Many places in Somerset have been cut off by the floods, and some of the phone lines are down. If that's where she went, she might have got stuck.'

With a wave of relief, Vicky said, 'of course! Thank you, officer, I expect that's what's happened.'

*

The roads in Perfect were in a terrible state and there was no sign of anyone from the Council coming to repair them. Landowners had to take matters into their own hands, and I spent the next day with Simon as he toured the family orchards, checking on the crops and the workers on the farm, organising repairs to fences and property damaged by the storm. He rode on horseback, and I climbed up onto the saddle behind him, dressed in some old clothes his mother had lent me, and although I'd never ridden before it felt like the most natural thing in the world.

I was impressed by how Simon dealt with people, being sympathetic and practical, and the locals seemed pleased to see me by his side. He told me that as an only child he was heir to his parents' farm and had been in training for this job all his life, then he turned to me with a winning smile and added, 'all I need now is a wife!'

We rode towards the edge of the village, passing some tall iron gates with a driveway leading to a large mansion. A team of labourers were busy, clearing the drive of fallen branches.

'Who lives there?' I asked.

'That's Denton Hall, Squire Marlow's home.'

'It looks huge. Does he have a family?'

'No, but he employs an army of servants to look after the house and grounds. He runs the village, so he's a busy man.'

After doing the rounds we returned to the stables where Simon dismounted and helped me down. Holding me in his arms he said, 'thanks for your support today, Beth, you've been magnificent!'

Then, we kissed – our first, proper, lingering kiss. I melted into his body, captivated by his gentle touch and tenderness, loving the sensation of being close to him, and knew at that moment, deep within me, that this was where I belonged, with this man, in this place.

*

In Bath the days passed, the floods subsided but still there was no sign of Beth. The police broke into her flat to search for clues as to where she might be and interviewed her neighbours, but no one could help. In response to an appeal, the owner of the restaurant where Beth and Simon had dined that Sunday evening came forward, saying that the couple had been totally absorbed in one another and paid in cash. Off-licences were approached in an effort to find Simon's friend Will, but there was no trace of him.

The police circulated details of the missing woman around the county and received reports of possible sightings, but nothing substantive, and in any case there was no proof that she had gone to Somerset at all – the young man could have taken her anywhere. It was hopeless. Beth seemed to have vanished into thin air.

At the café Vicky and her staff were in a terrible state, guilty that they'd left Beth with the stranger that night, missing her, at a loss as to how to find her, and fearing that something dreadful must have happened. On a practical note Vicky said, 'if she doesn't show up soon I'll have to take on someone else! We've been so busy lately.'

Andy the cook said, 'the only thing I don't miss is her singing – used to drive me daft!'

They laughed.

'I know what you mean,' said Vicky, 'all those verses of '*Barbara Allen*'! She does have a nice voice, though – remember that distinctive catch in her throat? I'd recognise it anywhere.'

*

Over the next days I assisted Simon with his work on the farm and helped his mother with the cooking, making pastries which everyone enjoyed. The Fairfax's introduced me to the villagers who were friendly and welcoming, and I fitted in well, even noticing people who looked like me, with similar colouring and build, and others who resembled Simon, with those lovely blue eyes and fair hair. I even met one woman who reminded me of my mother, and wondered if she might be a distant relation. I felt at home in Perfect, adapting to its arcane ways, my previous, modern life gradually fading from my mind.

Each day Simon and I grew more intimate, and one evening when he saw me to my room he came in, closed the door, and kissed me, fervently.

'I love you, Beth,' he said, holding me tight, running his hands deliciously down my back and over my generous hips.

'I love you too,' I said, caressing his strong, muscular body, our passion growing as we kissed again, but suddenly, he drew back and let me go.

'I'm sorry, Beth, I want you, desperately, but I can't, not yet. I think you're the loveliest girl I've ever met! It's just that we…my people, here…we don't believe in sex before marriage. It's the way I've been brought up, that it's better to wait. I know it sounds old-fashioned…'

I felt frustrated at being so abruptly let down, yet reassured that he really did want me.

'It's all right, I understand.'

'But I can't wait too long… Marry me, Beth! I want you to be my wife!'

I was swept away, thrilled to have found someone I loved, who loved me back, the best feeling in the world.

'Oh Simon! Yes, of course I'll marry you! I can't imagine my life without you!'

We kissed, again, then he left the room and I lay on the bed, my heart brimming with joy.

∗

Vicky was desperate to do anything she could to help find Beth, and when one of the officers investigating her disappearance mentioned that they'd found Beth's diary, Vicky asked to see it, hoping she might pick up a clue the police had missed. She borrowed the diary and took it home to read, feeling awkward, intruding upon Beth's private thoughts recorded in her familiar, neat handwriting (so good for writing up the daily menus on the board). She reached the last page where, rather than sentences, Beth had written the word 'Simon' several times over, alongside the word 'Perfect'.

Vicky closed the diary with resignation. So that was it: Beth had found her perfect man and gone away with him, but where, and would she ever come back?

*

When Simon and I announced our engagement his parents were delighted, and the whole village shared our happiness. Certain women came to congratulate me with a kiss on the cheek, followed by a knowing look which I didn't understand, but it didn't bother me: I'd never felt so happy in my life. Simon and I wanted to marry as soon as possible and quickly put all the arrangements in hand.

One fine evening in late October, just before our wedding, Simon said, 'come with me, there's something I want to show you,' and we rode to a place just outside the village with a beautiful view over the flat fields of the Somerset Levels, fading into the distance. We dismounted and sat down on the grass.

'It's lovely, but why have we come here?'

'Just wait and see.'

Slowly, as the sun lowered in the sky, we watched as some birds began to gather, then more came, and soon the air was alive with the chattering of thousands of starlings, mustering in the evening light. We watched, fascinated, as the birds whirled and swirled as one, drawing patterns in the sky, their wings beating as they flew overhead in their primeval dance.

'It's called a murmuration,' said Simon.

The mesmerising performance lasted several minutes, then the birds dispersed as quickly as they had gathered, and the sun set.

'That's amazing,' I said, in wonder.

'It is. Just think, Beth: the starlings have been massing like this for hundreds, maybe thousands of years, in this ancient landscape. The Levels are timeless. These marshes and fields have seen centuries of floods and fighting, but they will always survive.'

Taking his hands in mine he continued, 'Beth, I want you to understand that in marrying me you're committing to staying here, forever, away from the outside world. Are you willing to accept that?'

'I love you, Simon, and I love this place. Of course I want to stay here with you. Why would I want to be anywhere else, when everything here is perfect?'

Our wedding day was wonderful, the local church full of so much goodwill, I felt the whole village was pleased to receive me as one of their own. After the ceremony Simon and I moved to the village hall for the wedding breakfast where we greeted and thanked our guests. The men shook my hand and the women kissed me on the cheek, some of them giving me that strange look again. Then Marjorie embraced me and said, softly, so that no one else could hear, 'don't worry, my dear, he'll be gentle. Things will turn out all right, you'll see.'

I was surprised to hear such words from my mother-in-law, but she walked on before I could say anything.

The final guest to arrive was Squire Marlow, who until now had sat quietly at the back of the church, observing the proceedings. A hush descended as he entered the hall.

Simon went to him, bowed, and said, 'sir, I have the honour of presenting my wife, Mistress Beth Fairfax.'

I instinctively curtsied to this charismatic man and was rewarded with a nod and a smile. He took my hand and kissed it, staring into my eyes, and I was struck by his looks: for a man in his sixties he was handsome, with those same blue eyes that so many of the villagers had - including Simon; that same cut of the jawline, and fair hair, albeit thinning.

'Welcome to Perfect, Mistress Fairfax. We are delighted to have you amongst us.

Congratulations, Simon, you have chosen very well. And now,' he declared to the crowd, 'music!'

The fiddlers struck up and the rest of the day passed in a whirl of food, cider, dancing and singing, with many saying how much they liked my voice. In the evening people gradually left the hall until Simon and I were alone. We kissed, then he said, 'Beth, I have a surprise for you.'

I assumed we were going to spend the night at his parents' house, but outside the hall there was a horse, saddled up and ready to ride. Simon mounted and helped me up to sit behind him.

'This is exciting! Where are we going?'

'You'll see.'

In the moonlight we rode towards the edge of the village, then passed through some iron gates and up a driveway to a large mansion. I recognised it as Denton Hall, where Squire Marlow lived.

'Why have we come here?' I asked as we dismounted. Simon didn't reply, but knocked on the great door which the Squire himself answered, as if he were expecting us. He held out his hand to me and I took it, crossing the threshold, then turned and saw that Simon wasn't following me.

'Well done, boy,' said the Squire, 'a buxom red-head, just as I'd asked.'

Simon didn't speak, but bowed his head, said, 'goodnight, Beth. Until tomorrow,' and galloped away.

I looked after him, crying out, 'Simon! Don't leave me!', but he was gone.

The Squire placed his hands on my shoulders and cast his eyes over me, still dressed in my wedding gown.

'There's no reason to be afraid, Beth.'

'But I want to be with my husband!'

Laughing, he replied, 'you'll be with your husband for the rest of your life, but tonight, you're mine!'

With that he grabbed my wrist and pulled me towards the staircase. I screamed, 'let me go!' but the more I struggled to free myself from his firm grasp, the more he seemed to enjoy himself, reining me in as if he were taming a horse. He led me up the stairs, speaking softly, telling me I was a beautiful, strong lass and had nothing to fear.

I shouted out, 'it's Simon I want to be with, not you! It's our wedding night!'

He put his arms around me and said, 'that's why you're here! All the brides in the village are taken by me, first. Haven't you heard of the *droit du seigneur*?'

Now I understood the meaning of those odd looks from the women in the village. But Marjorie – had she suffered the same fate with this man? My mind distracted by the implications of this thought, I found myself in the Squire's bedchamber where he pushed me onto his bed and held me down until I stopped struggling. Then, he kissed me. I tried to resist – I really did – but he was overpowering and strong, yet gentle, murmuring endearments, and somehow, I found myself returning his kisses, surrendering to his desires.

'Make the most of your time with me, my dear,' he whispered, 'I'm a man of experience, after all. I'll teach you things tonight which will serve you well in the future...'

The next morning, Squire Marlow pulled back the heavy curtains, letting sunlight stream into the room, and I awoke from a deep, satisfying sleep. He was fully dressed, and threw some clothes onto the bed.

'Take these,' he said. 'You can't go home in your wedding gown.'

I sat up in bed, trying to remember where I was and what had happened…then it all came back to me…

'See, it wasn't so bad, was it? But my work is done, Beth. You belong to Simon now.'

He gave me breakfast, then fetched his horse, I climbed up behind him and we rode over to the farm where Simon came out to greet us. He held out his arms to embrace me, and with a loving smile we both forgave each other for what had happened the night before: Simon for abandoning me to Squire Marlow's seductive powers, and me for submitting to them. Simon nodded his respects to the Squire who rode away, then we entered the cottage, ready to begin our married life together.

Nine months to the day I gave birth to a beautiful, fair-haired boy, just like his father. My life in Perfect was complete.

*

Vicky was celebrating another birthday and it struck her that seven years had passed since that fateful night when Beth had disappeared. Thinking of her, she dug out the diary the police had let her keep, read the last entry yet again then sadly put it away.

The next weekend she paid her regular visit to Bath Antiques Market where she enjoyed browsing, picking up the odd treasure to decorate her home. She was chatting to one of the stall holders when she spotted a framed print of an ancient map of Somerset.

'It's a copper etching,' he said, 'it's really old - shows Somerset back in the seventeenth century.'

'Fascinating!' said Vicky, picking it up for inspection and appreciating the fine quality. 'I love it! How much?'

They agreed a price and Vicky put the map in her bag.

At home that evening, over a glass of wine, Vicky took out the map and examined it with a magnifying glass, and that was when she spotted it: in the Somerset Levels, near Glastonbury, there was a village called Perfect.

A shiver ran up her spine.

Beth had written the word in her diary. Was this what she had meant?

The thought nagged Vicky all night and she couldn't let it go. The next morning, she got up early and drove to the Levels, using the antique etching to try and locate Perfect as she couldn't find it on a modern road atlas. She spent hours driving through the marshy, flat landscape and along sunken, narrow country lanes bordered by high hedgerows, asking the occasional passer-by for directions, but could find no trace of such a place.

In the late afternoon, disappointed that her quest had been fruitless, she stopped by the edge of a small lake fringed with willow trees.

She got out the car to stretch her legs and was gazing at the calm, blue water, when she noticed an elderly man standing a few feet away from her. His face was weathered, his white beard untidy.

He looked at her and said, 'good day.'

Vicky smiled and said, 'hello.'

'Tranquil, that's what visitors say – it's tranquil.'

'It certainly is. You're local, then?'

'Born and bred, just up the road there.'

'You haven't by any chance heard of a village called Perfect?'

He raised his eyebrows. 'So why might you be asking that?'

'I think a friend of mine went there, but I've been searching all day and I can't find it, or her.'

The old man chuckled. 'Well, I'm not surprised. Perfect doesn't exist, but it's right in front of you.'

He was speaking in riddles and Vicky was growing impatient.

'What do you mean? It's important!'

He clammed up and looked over the lake.

'I'm sorry, I didn't mean to snap, but I'm worried about my friend. She disappeared seven years ago and my only clue is that she wrote the word 'Perfect' in her diary. I saw it on an old map, but I've been looking all day and can't find it. Please tell me what you know!'

Seeing her exasperation, the old man took a deep breath and, speaking in his rich Somerset burr, began his tale.

'Centuries ago there were many villages on the Levels, but over the years the floods swept them away – farmland, livestock, people, houses, all lost. But they say that some survived, deep down in lakes like this one. Perfect was one of those villages.'

A wave of understanding slowly flowed over her.

'You mean, Perfect is still here, but under the water?'

'That's right.'

He paused, then said, 'legend has it that once a year, on Michaelmas Day, a young man from Perfect is chosen to come ashore to seek a bride and take her back with him, to introduce new blood. And sometimes, on a calm evening like this, if you listen carefully, you can hear the village come alive, beneath the surface…'

Vicky nodded her thanks and turned away from the old man who ambled away. Left alone, she stood for a long time, staring at the expanse of still water.

As she looked and listened she gradually became aware of signs of life: people talking, children laughing, horses neighing, the hustle and bustle of village life. Then she heard, quite clearly, the strains of an old folk song.

The catch in the singer's voice was unmistakeable.

It was Beth, singing '*Barbara Allen*.'

OLD DOG

'But Dad, we just don't do it like that anymore! You've got to get up-to-date, move with the times. We're in the twenty-first century now, you know!'

The old man sighed and wiped his eyes.

'I'm sure you're right son, but it's hard for us old'uns…I feel as if all the skills I've got are useless. And it's so difficult to learn new things when you're older - you know, old dogs, new tricks…'

'Look, I can help you – just like you used to help me when I was starting out.'

'Yes…I remember, they were good days, back then…'

He smiled, thinking of the past, of his youth, but couldn't dwell on it long because his son said, 'now, come and sit yourself down.'

His father sat down heavily on a swivel chair in front of a computer and peered at the screen.

'There, make yourself comfortable so you can use the mouse and the keyboard, and I'll show you what to do.'

'All right, I'm as ready as I'll ever be.'

'Good. So, you press this key and in a minute the details of the bank account will come up. I've done all the prep and everything's ready.'

'It just doesn't seem right, though…'

'Aw come on, you can't have reservations now – not at this stage! It's no different from what you used to do – and a hell of a lot safer!'

'I suppose so…'

The old man looked at the three remaining fingers on his right hand. His son followed his gaze and said, 'exactly. No gelignite, no safe cracking, no noise, no get-away cars, no blown-off fingers. And you don't even have to leave the house. Trust me.'

The old man fidgeted in his chair.

'I know…but it just seems…'

He hesitated, his mind full of doubts.

'…it seems unfair, somehow, to nick the stuff from – well, real people. I mean, the Bank is an institution, isn't it. The Bank is…THEM.

Whereas this…' he said, pointing at the screen full of figures, 'this is personal. This is more like…US.'

The son looked at his father.

'I know what you mean, Dad. But you have to face the facts - the truth stares you in the face every time you walk down the High Street. THERE AREN'T ANY MORE BANKS!'

The old man nodded his head slowly.

'That's what they call progress, eh? Okay then, son, you win. Show me how this 'hacking' works…'

ADELAIDE'S STORY

London, 1888

The woman was working her way along the dark, dirty, foul-smelling street in Paddington, handing out chunks of bread to the needy, when she noticed a girl huddled in the shelter of a doorway, her shawl wrapped around her against the cold night.

'Have something to eat, dear.'

The girl looked up, mumbled, 'thank you, Miss,' eagerly took the bread and stuffed it into her mouth.

The woman hadn't seen her on her patch before and asked, 'how long have you been living like this?'

'About a month I s'pose.'

'And you don't have anywhere to go?'

'No. My stepmother threw me out and nobody wants me.'

'How old are you?'

'Sixteen, Miss.'

In the dim light of the gas lamp the woman could see that the girl was dishevelled and filthy, but had an honest face and was wearing a decent pair of boots – she hadn't been homeless for long and there was time to rescue her before her situation worsened. She helped the girl, who was of slight build, onto her feet.

'I'm Matron Jones and I run a home for people like yourself. Come with me, you'll be safe there. What's your name?'

'Adelaide Robinson.'

Adelaide was wary, but instinct told her she could trust this woman, and anything was better than spending another night on the streets. Cold, tired and hungry, with nothing to lose, she followed Matron Jones to the Home for Destitute Women, a dismal, soot-blackened terraced building at the back of the railway station. Matron took Adelaide down to the basement kitchen, the one room where the fire was always lit, gave her some soup, and filled a tin bath with hot water.

'Clean yourself up. There's an empty room upstairs where you can stay. Get some sleep and I'll speak to you in the morning.'

'Thank you, Miss.'

Left alone, Adelaide got into the bath and gave herself a good scrub, the water turning black with dirt and grime from her body and hair, then dried herself off, relieved to be clean again. She put on the nightdress Matron had left her, lit a candle, found her way to her room and collapsed on the bed in exhaustion.

When Adelaide awoke the next morning, she put on the clean clothes she found at the foot of the bed and went down to the kitchen where a dozen or so women were seated around the table having breakfast. They glanced up at her but didn't speak. Adelaide helped herself from the pot of porridge on the stove, then Matron called her to the office where she made a note of the newcomer's details and asked about her circumstances.

'I lived in Limehouse with my parents,' Adelaide began. 'My Pa's a shipwright at the docks, and Ma looked after us all. My older brothers left to join the Army, so I was the last one at home. Then three years ago Ma got ill and I had to leave school to care for her. Pa was always kind to us, but when Ma died he found it hard and started drinking. He took up with a horrible woman he met at the tavern and last year they got married and she moved in with us.'

Adelaide's mood quickly turned from sorrow to anger.

'I hate her! She was widowed and had some money, but they drank it away. At home she expected me to do all the work, but she beat me and kept it from Pa, and when I told him he didn't believe me. One night he hit me, and he'd never laid a finger on me before, not all these years. About a month ago we had this big argument and she chucked me out, the cow!'

'And there's no prospect of you going back?'

'Never!'

'And you have no other relatives you could stay with?'

'No.'

Matron looked at Adelaide, seeing a decent girl who was genuinely aggrieved and worthy of assistance.

'You can stay here for the time being, Miss Robinson. You'll have to earn your keep, but you'll be fed and have a roof over your head.'

'Thank you, Matron, I'm much obliged.'

Adelaide struggled to understand how she had sunk so low, but there was no turning back – she could never go home again, too many terrible things had been said and done, and it broke her heart to think what her Ma would have made of it all. For the moment she was grateful for Matron Jones' help and determined to make the best of her situation.

Over the next weeks Adelaide regained her strength, helping with the chores, working alongside the other inmates - alcoholics, pregnant women, beggars, each with a story to tell, each with nowhere else to go. Regular meals helped her gain weight, restoring the colour to her face, and with her wide brown eyes and long, chestnut-brown hair there were signs of the pretty girl she had once been.

Matron made discreet enquiries which confirmed what Adelaide had related regarding her family circumstances. She wanted to set the girl on the right path, and when she felt sure she was ready to move on, called Adelaide into her office.

'I've found a position for you as a living-in servant with a Mr and Mrs Dean in Surrey. I've told them about your background and said you're honest and a hard worker. I'll provide your rail fare and you can catch the train down there tomorrow. They'll be expecting you.'

'Thank you, Matron, I appreciate it.'

'Good. Now, don't let me down,' she said, handing Adelaide a piece of paper with details of the Deans' address.

Surrey, 1888

Adelaide had never left the capital, so it was in a state of nervous excitement that she boarded a train for the first time, bound for Caterham. It was a warm, sunny day in May and as they steamed into the Surrey countryside she stared out the window, enthralled, as buildings and factories were replaced by green hills and meadows where sheep and cows were grazing, just like the picture book her mother used to read to her.

At Caterham she disembarked, breathing in unfamiliar fresh air as she walked through the quiet market town and up the hill to the Dean's home, Drayford House, with its two distinctive gables and tall chimneys. She went round the back to the tradesmen's entrance and knocked on the door to be met by Mrs York, the cook.

'My name's Adelaide Robinson, the new servant.'

'Come in, dear. I've just made a pot of tea – would you like some?'

Grateful for the friendly reception, Adelaide sat down at the kitchen table while Mrs York asked about her journey and told her about the household.

'We're a small staff – there's just me and

my husband, and another servant, Iris. Mr and Mrs Dean are retired and their son lives here with his wife and two young children. Mrs Dean does a lot of charity work and keeps in touch with her friends in London – that will be how she found out about you.'

They finished drinking their tea, then Cook took Adelaide upstairs to the drawing room to meet Mrs Dean, a kindly lady in her seventies, who welcomed her, saying, 'you were recommended on good authority, Miss Robinson. Work well, and we'll look after you.'

Cook showed Adelaide to an attic room in one of the gable ends which she was to share with Iris. Her new uniform of a long black dress, white apron and white cap was laid out on the bed.

'It ought to fit you all right. I serve supper for the staff at six, so come downstairs at five and you can give me a hand.'

That night, Adelaide lay awake in the silent house, reflecting on the events of the last months. She wondered whether she should write and tell her father where she was but decided against it, knowing that her old life in Limehouse was gone forever. She was grateful for the help she'd received from Matron Jones and pleased to get away from London.

Drayford House was her new home and she was glad of it - the Deans seemed a pleasant family, the staff were friendly and she liked Iris, a shy, country girl a little younger than Adelaide.

At five the next morning, Iris woke her new room-mate and took her down to the kitchen where Cook and her husband were having breakfast.

'You look tired, Adelaide,' said Cook. 'Did you sleep all right?'

'Not really. It was so quiet, I couldn't settle! Then there was this bright light, like a big lamp outside my window. Kept me awake, it did!'

They looked at her and Mr York sniggered.

'You silly thing!' said Cook, 'it was the moon!'

Adelaide grew used to her daily tasks, rising early to lay the fires in the house and sweep up ashes from the night before, empty the chamberpots, make the beds, scrub the floors, polish the silver and brass, do the washing and help in the kitchen, all for a meagre wage. But there were benefits, notably Cook's wholesome food, and the staff were allowed one afternoon off a month.

On Sunday mornings the whole household went to Church, Adelaide and Iris wearing second-hand but smart clothes which Mrs Dean provided for them. When Adelaide turned seventeen in June, she determined that the worst of her life was behind her; she was pretty, in good health, and happy with her lot.

The months passed quickly and after a harsh Winter, Spring arrived. One day she was in the kitchen with Cook who was awaiting a delivery of flour from the local corn merchants. They heard a horse and cart draw up, there was a knock on the back door and a good-looking man, aged about twenty, entered, carrying a sack of flour on his back.

'Mornin' Mrs York,' he said, as Cook greeted him and opened the door to the pantry where the flour was stored. He was strong, of medium height, with a shock of thick dark hair and a charming smile.

'Sit down and have some tea, you need something after all that hard work!' said Cook. 'Adelaide, cut him a slice of cake.'

Adelaide did so and he winked at her, making her feel self-conscious.

'You're new, aren't you? I don't remember seeing your pretty face before.'

She blushed.

'I've been here nearly a year!'

'Really? Mrs York must have been hiding you away! So, what's your name?'

'Adelaide.'

'Adelaide…a pretty name for a pretty girl…'

He looked at her and laughed at her embarrassment.

'Thomas Cooling, at your service.'

She nodded and watched while he scoffed his cake, brushing away crumbs from his mouth with the back of his hand. He finished and got up.

'Thank you, Mrs York - and I'll look forward to seeing you again, Adelaide.'

After he left, Cook said, 'he's a charmer. Don't take any notice of him.'

When Thomas made his next delivery he spotted Adelaide in the garden, hanging out the washing, and went to speak to her. She led a quiet life and knew no one outside the house, and despite Cook's warning she was flattered by his attention. He chatted amiably, then asked when she had her time off.

'It'll be next Sunday afternoon.'

'Perfect! Meet me in town after Church and we can go for a walk.'

When the day came Adelaide put on her Sunday best - a long blue woollen skirt, white high-necked blouse, a Paisley pattern shawl around her shoulders and her hair up – and Thomas greeted her with a warm smile.

'My, you look lovely today! May I walk with you?'

As they strolled through the quiet streets Thomas told her about himself and showed her the corn merchants where he worked.

'I'm the corn dealer's assistant,' he said, proudly. 'I do all the deliveries and Mr Tutt, the owner, wants to teach me the business.'

Adelaide didn't talk about her past life, preferring to enjoy the present moment and the company of the handsome young man. At the end of the afternoon they returned to Drayford House where Thomas said goodbye and asked to see her again, and she accepted. That Summer, during which Adelaide had her eighteenth birthday, Thomas drove her around the country roads in his horse and cart, she listening as he talked about his ambitions, although he showed little interest in hers. At night, Iris would quiz her about what they'd been doing.

'Has he kissed you?'

'No! We're just friends,' Adelaide replied, although, she did wonder what it would be like to be kissed.

In the harvest season Thomas was too busy to see her, then it was Winter again, with days too cold and rainy to venture out. It was in the Spring of the next year that Mrs Dean sent Adelaide into town on an errand. While at the haberdasher's she spotted Thomas in the distance, driving his horse and cart, but this time, someone else was sitting up next to him – a pretty girl with fair hair. As the cart approached, Adelaide stayed in the shelter of the shop and watched as they rode past. She saw the couple laughing together, engrossed in each other's company, and felt a pang of jealousy. She was upset, but said nothing for fear of looking foolish.

When Thomas next came to the house delivering flour, Adelaide deliberately ignored him, but he approached her, put his hand under her chin and lifted her face up to his.

'What's wrong, my pretty Adelaide?'

She refused to say at first, but he cajoled her until she said, 'I saw you with a fair-haired girl in your cart. Are you walking out with her?'

'I don't know who you mean!'

'A few weeks ago, when I was at the haberdasher's, I saw you. Don't deny it!'

Thomas looked thoughtful, then said, 'ah, I remember! She's a friend of my sister and I was driving her over to see her.'

'Really?'

'Yes! I hope you're not jealous!'

'Of course not!'

'You have no reason to be – and that's why, my pretty girl, I want you to come with me to the May Day fair.'

'Oh!'

By tradition, servants were given leave to join the May Day celebrations, but Adelaide hadn't expected Thomas to ask her to go with him. Overcoming her annoyance, she accepted his invitation.

On May Day, Adelaide met Thomas on the green where the festivities were taking place. He was looking smart, wearing his best trousers and a waistcoat over a linen shirt, and when he offered her his arm she was pleased to take it. Together they wandered around the fair, looking at the sights and watching the Morris dancers, then Thomas said, 'stay here, I'll go and fetch us some drinks.'

Adelaide sat on the grass, watching Thomas as he walked to the refreshment tent, admiring his easy, confident manner, greeting men he knew with a smile and a slap on the back. He returned with two glasses of beer.

'Oh! I haven't drunk beer before!' Adelaide exclaimed.

'Well, it's time you did! Cheers!'

She took a sip, finding the bitterness unpleasant, but she was thirsty and finished the glass, by which time she was growing used to the taste and readily accepted another which she drank quickly. Thomas was on his way to fetch more beer when he was approached by the fair-haired woman Adelaide had seen him with in town. She watched the two talking, glancing in her direction, and knew she shouldn't have trusted what Thomas had told her. Feeling angry and upset she got up and began walking back to Drayford House, but Thomas saw her leave and ran after her, catching her up in a quiet lane.

'Wait, Adelaide, please wait!'

He caught her by the shoulders and turned her to face him.

'I'm sorry, I didn't know she'd be there. But it's you I want, Adelaide, not her. I want you to be my girl.'

'But I don't want you.'

'Please, forgive me, my pretty Adelaide – come on… be mine…'

He slipped his arms around her waist, drew her to him and kissed her. She tried to wriggle free, but he persisted, and the combination of his warm kisses and the after-effects of the beer made her feel light-headed. Despite her misgivings, she found herself responding to his caresses and when he whispered, 'come lie with me,' she let him lead her into a field away from view where they lay on the grass and kissed again, then he lifted her skirts and fumbled with her undergarments. She pushed his hand away.

'You haven't been with a man before, have you?'

She wasn't sure what he meant.

'Adelaide, if you really want to be my girl then you've got to let me…'

He was beginning to scare her, yet she didn't want to lose him, so let him touch her. He grew excited, then the next thing she knew he was on top of her, moving, and it was painful, his breathing grew rapid, he gave out a gasp, then it was over, and he rolled off onto the grass. They lay there for a moment while he recovered his breath, she struggling to grasp what had happened, then he got up, held out his hand and pulled her to her feet. She smoothed down her skirts and looked at him.

'Am I your girl now?'

He put his hands on her shoulders and laughed at her.

'My poor, sweet Adelaide,' he said, kissed her on her forehead, then turned and walked away, back to the fair.

Confused and distressed, Adelaide returned to Drayford House and told no one about her encounter with Thomas.

On her next afternoon off Cook asked, 'aren't you walking out with your young man?'

'No – I don't want to see him anymore.'

But she did see him several times in town, driving his cart, with the fair-haired girl sitting beside him. It really hurt, and she vowed to have nothing more to do with him.

In the Autumn, Adelaide realised she was putting on weight. It started with Mr York teasing her, saying, 'have you been scoffing too much of my wife's cake?' Her clothes were tight, and she realised she hadn't needed to use the rags for a while. Cook noticed and took her to one side to ask how she was.

'I'm a bit tired, to be honest. And my clothes don't seem to fit any more.'

Cook took her hand and said, gently, 'do you think you could be with child?'

Adelaide was shocked and didn't understand.

'Did you lie with Thomas?'

Remembering that afternoon, she said, 'yes, after the May Day fair. He told me if I didn't I wouldn't be his girl – but afterwards we never met again.'

'Oh Adelaide, you silly, silly girl! I think you might be in trouble…'

The truth began to dawn.

'I didn't know! I didn't realise… Oh, Cook, what am I going to do?'

'I'll talk to Mrs Dean – she'll find a way to help you. Now, don't you worry…'

Mrs Dean was shocked, and at first doubted whether Adelaide had really been ignorant of her situation. However, when she spoke to her she could see from the girl's distress that she was genuine.

'You're sure it was Thomas Cooling?'

'Yes! I haven't been with anybody else!'

Mrs Dean thought for a moment. 'I'll write to my friend Mrs Shaw in London and ask her advice - she runs a charity for women.'

'Thank you, Mrs Dean – I'm sorry to cause so much trouble…'

Adelaide began to cry.

'Now, now dear,' said Mrs Dean, passing her a handkerchief, 'I'll do what I can. You're not the first and you won't be the last…'

Adelaide passed a miserable Christmas, then in the new year Mrs Dean called her into the drawing room. She held a letter in her hand.

'I've received a response from Mrs Shaw. She has very kindly made an appointment for you to see a doctor at a hospital in London, next week. I will accompany you. She's also arranged a place for you at a home in Hackney where you'll be able to stay until you have the baby.'

'Thank you. But can't I come back here? I've been so happy - until this…'

Mrs Dean took a deep breath, her patience waning.

'Miss Robinson, you must understand, this changes everything! You can't live at Drayford House with a baby! You wouldn't be able to work *and* look after it, and my husband and our family have our reputation to think of. We can't have an unmarried mother living under our roof.'

'I'm sorry, Mrs Dean, I hadn't thought of it like that…'

Adelaide was devastated. It was all so unfair – she hadn't meant to lie with Thomas, and she certainly hadn't wanted a baby. She felt helpless, and saw no alternative but to go along with Mrs Dean's proposal.

London, 1891

With sadness and regret, one cold January morning Adelaide left Drayford House and travelled to London with Mrs Dean, hating to leave the place she had come to regard as home and having to return to the noise and dirt of the capital.

They walked through the hectic, filthy streets piled with horse dung, and teeming with people. At the Middlesex hospital the doctor examined the patient, declared that she was indeed pregnant, and that the baby was due within the month.

Mrs Dean asked, 'but how could her pregnancy have remained hidden for so long?'

'I don't know,' replied the doctor, 'but cases like this do happen – only last week we had a girl here in the morning suffering from indigestion and at the end of the day she gave birth. She had no idea!'

Leaving the hospital, Mrs Dean said, 'now I'll take you to the home in Hackney. I know Miss Lavender, the Matron in charge. She'll look after you from now on.'

The Refuge for the Destitute was as bleak as its name, an austere four-storey terraced building in a deprived area run by the Female Aid Society. Mrs Dean and Adelaide entered the reception room where a fire was lit, the only spark of comfort in the cheerless house. Miss Lavender, a formidable but kind woman in her late fifties, welcomed Mrs Dean who introduced Adelaide and explained her circumstances. Then, with sorrow, Mrs Dean said her farewells and left her former servant in Matron's care.

Adelaide had only been at the Refuge a matter of weeks when she felt unwell and Matron said, 'it's your time.' She took her to Hackney hospital where the nurses had so many patients to attend to that Adelaide spent much of her long labour alone, crying out in agony, wanting her mother, railing against the world and Thomas, who'd got her into this situation, and cursing herself for her own ignorance. Finally, on the 5th February 1891, at the age of nineteen, she gave birth to a small but healthy baby boy. She named him Stanley Robinson.

Mother and son returned to the Refuge where the nursing staff showed Adelaide how to feed, bathe and change the newborn. Adelaide feared she might resent the baby, but as soon as the midwife placed him in her arms she instantly adored him. Little Stanley filled her with delight; every smile, holding him close, brushing her lips against the top of his head, breathing in the scent of him - she treasured it all. At last she had someone of her own to love, someone to pour her heart into.

Matron asked Adelaide about the baby's father, and listened attentively while Adelaide recalled her May Day encounter with Thomas.

'And this young man knows nothing of you and the baby?'

'No – unless Mrs Dean has told him.'

'Young men like Thomas must be made to face up to their responsibilities! Did he ever speak of marriage?'

'No – although I wouldn't want to marry him, anyway.'

Miss Lavender considered the situation.

'I believe you have been sadly wronged by this man. I'm going to pay him a visit.'

True to her word, Miss Lavender caught the train to Caterham and found Thomas at the corn merchants.

'I'm a friend of Miss Adelaide Robinson. I believe you know her.'

Thomas shrugged.

'Never heard of her.'

'But yes – she was a servant at Drayford House. You met her several times and walked out together.'

'No, I don't remember her.'

Miss Lavender had to contain her growing anger with this insolent young man.

'Now, listen to me – you left this poor woman pregnant with your child! She has given birth to a son and they need your help!'

Mr Tutt, the merchant, hearing the raised voices, came in and asked, 'what's all this about?'

Miss Lavender explained but Mr Tutt took Thomas's side.

'If he says he doesn't know the girl, then he doesn't know her. Now, I don't need some interfering old woman coming here disturbing my employees so will you kindly leave?'

Angry at the rebuttal, Miss Lavender left the merchants and went to Drayford House to find Mrs Dean, who listened in despair.

'I confronted Thomas as well and he told me the same story. He's lying, of course! We all know that he walked out with Adelaide. I've discussed the matter with my husband, and he has a suggestion. I'd be grateful if you could convey this to her...'

Back in Hackney, Adelaide asked, 'so what's an Affiliation Order?'

'It's a legal document,' Miss Lavender explained. 'It means that a man who is judged to be the father of an illegitimate child must help to support it. Adelaide, this is your chance to take Thomas to court, make him acknowledge that he is Stanley's father and force him to pay towards his upkeep.'

'My goodness! And Mr Dean would pay the legal fees?'

'Yes – he and Mrs Dean believe Thomas should face justice. You'll struggle to earn enough money to look after Stanley on your own. Most women in your position have to give up their babies permanently, unless they can find a husband - but not many men will take on a woman with an illegitimate child. I wish it were different, Adelaide, but it's how things are.'

The thought of giving up Stanley made Adelaide's blood run cold.

'I'll take Thomas to court and get every penny I can!'

The date was set and the case heard at Dalston Police Court in Hackney at the beginning of March. Adelaide approached the courtroom nervously, grateful for Miss Lavender's support. She was pleased to see Mr Dean there, and the counsel he employed gave an accurate account of Adelaide's situation. To their frustration, Thomas Cooling failed to attend court in person. His legal representative admitted that Thomas had met Adelaide at Drayford House, but said he hadn't seen her for two years and couldn't be the father of her baby.

To Adelaide's dismay, due to the lack of corroborative evidence, the Magistrate accepted Cooling's version of events and ruled that he would not be required to give any financial support towards the baby's care.

With a curt 'case dismissed', the Magistrate left the courtroom, leaving Adelaide devastated. Miss Lavender led her away, trying to shield her from the harsh, critical bystanders looking in scorn at the fallen woman who had given birth out of wedlock. Adelaide imagined Thomas' counsel returning victoriously to Caterham, having a celebratory drink with him, while she was left to bear the stigma of being an unmarried mother. The charming young man she had once liked had become a callous monster who showed no interest in his own son and certainly didn't care for her. She was grateful for the support of Miss Lavender and the Deans, who shared her indignation that Thomas had got away scot-free, but the question remained: with insufficient means to keep herself and her child, what was she to do?

Miss Lavender had a proposal.

'I've managed to find you a job – it's a living-in situation at a house in Finsbury Park. There's a foster home for Stanley nearby and you'll be able to visit him once a month. It's the best I can find for you in the circumstances.'

'Thank you – but can't I stay here?' Adelaide asked, plaintively.

'I'm sorry, but no, you can't – if we let everyone stay we'd have no room for all the women who'll need our help in the future.'

Adelaide regretfully left the Refuge, carrying a bag with the few possessions she had. She took Stanley to the foster mother who seemed a kind sort, but Adelaide was distressed at having to leave her precious baby, barely six weeks old, with a stranger.

'It's all right, dear, my lot will make a fuss of him, they like the new babies,' she said, gesturing to her own children, playing in the kitchen. 'You can come and see him at the end of the month. Don't worry, it will fly by!'

Adelaide put on a brave face and made her way to Finsbury Park, already missing her son desperately. She found the house, went to the tradesmen's entrance and rang the bell. A manservant answered the door and looked her up and down with a critical eye.

'You'll be the new maid. You'd better come in.'

Adelaide's duties were much the same as those she had undertaken at Drayford House, but the staff were unkind to her, making snide remarks about her situation. Doing her best to ignore them she threw herself into her work, tiring herself out to distract from thoughts of her baby. At the end of March on her afternoon off she made her first visit, feeling a rush of emotion as she clasped her son, noticing how much he'd grown.

Stanley cried with all the attention, and by the time mother and child were settled in each other's company it was time for her to leave, the foster mother practically having to force her out of the house.

Adelaide counted the days to her visits, aching to see Stanley, trying to fit a whole month's love into a few hours, and hated parting from him. Walking back to Finsbury Park in the rain she was hit by the reality that her wages went entirely towards the foster mother's fees of five shillings per week, leaving her with nothing, not even the fare for the omnibus. Unable to see a way out of her predicament, she paid a visit to Miss Lavender who listened sympathetically, but told her the harsh truth.

'A woman in your position will always struggle to cover the cost of foster care. It was worth a try, but I fear this arrangement isn't doing you or Stanley any good. I know it sounds hard, but quite honestly, it's better for everyone to make the situation permanent.'

Quietly, Adelaide uttered, 'you think I should give him up.'

Miss Lavender sighed.

'You must not think about yourself, but what is best for Stanley. I suggest you apply to the Foundling Hospital in Holborn for help -

they would provide for his long-term care and wellbeing, and it would give you both the opportunity for a new start.'

Over the next weeks, Adelaide turned the idea over in her mind and a feeling of dread descended upon her. The thought of parting with her child for good was unbearable, but it wasn't tenable to go on as she was - her brief visits distressed him and left her in pieces. Matron's words rang in her ears – it was Stanley's future that mattered. What could she offer him? A hand-to-mouth existence, heading for the workhouse. She had to set her own feelings aside and put Stanley first. With a leaden heart, she went to see Miss Lavender.

'I don't think I have a choice. I'll have to ask the Foundling Hospital to take Stanley. Please will you help me?'

Adelaide made her application and was invited to a meeting with the Hospital governors. In a state of high anxiety, Adelaide walked to Holborn, stood at the end of the wide driveway leading up to the imposing eighteenth century buildings, and froze. How could she possibly bring her treasured baby here and abandon him?

A group of boys of around nine years old passed her, talking and laughing together.

They certainly looked happy enough – clean, smartly-dressed, well-fed, well-spoken, on their way to their classes and sports. She tried to imagine her little Stanley at that age, living at the Hospital, going about with his friends... he would undoubtedly have a better quality of life here than she would ever be able to provide.

Her heart thumping, she continued up the driveway, found the committee room and entered nervously to find the chairman of the governors, flanked by two colleagues, seated behind a vast desk. He welcomed her and invited her to sit down.

'Miss Robinson, we have examined your application to have your son, Stanley, submitted into our care. You have strong references from Matron Lavender, a lady we know well and who has confirmed to us that you are an honest girl who has led a hard-working life. We have also received excellent references concerning your good character from your former employers Mr and Mrs Dean. Our enquiries have persuaded us that you are deserving of our help.'

Adelaide nodded and listened.

'For our part, we can assure you that if you put your son into our care he will be given the best possible start in life. We will place him with a foster family until he is five years old, then he will return to us to live and be schooled. We believe strongly in education and training, and he will receive the best. Now, you must understand, Miss Robinson, that once you hand your son to us you cannot have any further contact with him, nor will you be allowed to make any enquiries about him. We will give him a new name in order to protect both of you and give you both a fresh start. Is that clear?'

'Yes.'

'Reflect upon what we have said, and I am confident you will come to accept that this is the best course of action you can take for your son. Do you have any questions?'

Adelaide was stunned, trying to take in all the information. The Chairman looked at her over his spectacles.

'Miss Robinson?'

She shook her head.

'Very well. Let us know what you decide.'

Adelaide returned to Finsbury Park, her mind in a whirl. She would miss her son as surely as if a limb were cut off, but she mustn't think about her own selfish wants and needs; Stanley's future was at stake. The only currency she had was a mother's love, but love alone wouldn't feed and clothe him. Things were difficult now with him as a baby, but how would she cope as he grew older? She thought of the happy, healthy children she'd seen at the Hospital, with all the advantages that a solid education could bring – benefits which were totally out of her reach. After many sleepless nights of deep reflection, Adelaide went to see Miss Lavender.

'It breaks my heart to say it, but I've decided to admit Stanley to the Hospital.'

Miss Lavender nodded and took Adelaide's hands in hers, in sympathy and understanding.

'I'm going to hand in my notice and fetch Stanley from his foster mother. Please, can we stay here with you until it's done?'

Adelaide eyes were full of such distress that Miss Lavender couldn't refuse.

'Yes, my dear, until it's done.'

On the 23rd June 1891, when he was nearly five months old, Adelaide brought Stanley to the Foundling Hospital for admission. At the reception room she was met by a tight-lipped nurse who indicated a chair and said, 'Miss Robinson, please sit down and we'll complete the paperwork.'

Placing Stanley on her lap, her stomach tied in knots, Adelaide took a deep breath.

With a shaking hand she signed the necessary documents, placing her son permanently into the Hospital's care. She gave the nurse a bag, saying, 'here are some vests, and a cardigan I knitted him…and his favourite toy, a rattle…'

'Thank you,' said the nurse, putting the items to one side. 'I'll take him, then.'

The nurse held out her arms, expectantly. Adelaide felt numb inside. She couldn't move.

'When you're ready.'

I'll never be ready, she thought.

Adelaide looked down at Stanley who smiled up at her, and she crumpled.

'I can't! I can't!'

Her voice shook and the tears that had been welling up inside her, ran down her face.

'But you must! You can't change your mind now - you've signed the documents. It's the right thing to do for your baby's future.'

Adelaide, sobbing, clung tightly to her son who began to cry.

'Now you're making him distressed! Give him to me and he'll settle down.'

'NO! I won't!'

Adelaide bolted up from her chair which fell backwards with a crash and made for the door. One of the Governors was passing and heard the commotion. He recognised Adelaide from when she had appeared in front of the Committee, and barred her way.

'Miss Robinson, isn't it?' he said, calmly. 'You made the right decision, bringing your son to us. He couldn't be in better hands. Now, give him to me.'

The tighter she held her baby the louder he cried.

'Let me take him and he'll quieten down.'

The nurse came behind Adelaide and restrained her by the shoulders. Firmly, the Governor put his hands under the baby and extracted him from his mother's grasp.

'That's better,' he said, handing him to the nurse.

Adelaide made to grab her son as the nurse left the room, but the Governor put out his arm to restrain her and she let out a gut-wrenching scream, watching helplessly as her baby disappeared from view, down the corridor and out of her life forever.

Somehow, Adelaide got herself back to the Refuge. She ran up to her room, passing Miss Lavender but unable to speak. She threw herself onto the bed, weeping, hugging her knees tight to her body, drowning in a sea of anguish. Lost in her world of desperation the hours passed and still her tears would not stop.

Of course she had done the right thing, giving up her baby – everybody told her so. But now it was done she knew for certain that she would never get over her loss. The hollowness she felt inside, that hole in her heart, would stay with her forever, and there would never be a day when she wouldn't think of her son, hoping he was safe, missing him, loving him…

And as her thoughts wandered, a desperate question filled her mind.

What shall I do now?

*

Author's Note

Adelaide's story is based on true events.

On the day Stanley Robinson was admitted into the care of the Foundling Hospital he was baptised and given a new name by which he was known for the rest of his life. He was looked after by foster carers until the age of five when he was returned to the Foundling Hospital where he lived until the age of fifteen. In his leaving reference, the headmaster described him as, 'an excellent boy, very trustworthy and a thorough worker.'

He joined the Royal Navy and served during the Great War. He married, and he and his wife had a daughter who married my uncle.

Some years after her father's death my aunt contacted the Thomas Coram Foundation, which is responsible for managing the legacy of the Foundling Hospital, to enquire about her father's background, and that is how Adelaide's story came to light.

Despite extensive research I have been unable to find out for certain what happened to Adelaide after she gave up her son. She may have married and had a family. Equally, she may have suffered the fate that so many women in her position at that time endured: to end her days in the workhouse.

EPIPHANY

My husband complained that the star on the top of our Christmas tree wasn't very bright (it needs a new battery). I said, 'what do you expect, shepherds and the three wise men?'

But now Epiphany has been and gone; we have celebrated the visit of the Magi to the Christ child and stowed the decorations away for another year. Epiphany - Twelfth Night - is celebrated in different ways in different parts of the world. In France, they serve a delicious frangipane pie called *Galette des Rois*, topped with a golden paper crown. The pie contains a small porcelain figure and the lucky person who finds it is crowned King for the day and gets to wear the crown (hoping they haven't broken a tooth on said porcelain figure).

In Italy, Befana, a little, bent-over old woman, delivers presents to children from the sack she carries on her back. In Poland the feast day is celebrated in style, all the more so since 2011 when the 6th January was restored as a national public holiday for the first time since it was cancelled under communism fifty years earlier.

The word 'epiphany' doesn't only apply to a particular date, though. The word is used colloquially to represent a key moment in a person's life: that illuminating instant when they realise their destiny, who they truly love, an intuitive understanding of what they have been put on the planet for. In a film or book it is that pivotal moment of discovery when everything makes sense, evoking emotions which make you catch your breath or cry. An epiphany can change your whole life.

When was yours?

SECRETS, SPONGES AND SPIES

London, 1963

'This cake is delicious!' said Nigel, waving his fork in the air, 'what on earth did you put in it?'

'I can't possibly tell you', said Mary, 'it's my family's secret recipe. If I tell you I'll have to kill you.'

'I'll just have to keep guessing then,' he said, putting down his empty plate. 'Honestly though, that was great, thanks, I can't survive a Sunday afternoon without cake. And some you-know-what...'

He pulled her towards him, kissed her and she giggled as he expertly unzipped her dress. It fell to the floor, and they fell onto the bed.

In the early morning light Mary lay half-asleep, watching her lover as he struggled to find his clothes and get dressed without disturbing her. He had to be in his office in Whitehall by 7am, but she had the luxury of another hour of rest before she had to get to work. The light glinted on the gold braid of his Royal Navy uniform as he bent over to kiss her.

'Goodbye sweetheart, see you soon,' he whispered, and was gone.

She got ready for the day, dressing in a fashionably short skirt and top, then brushed her long, fair hair and put on her makeup. Satisfied with how she looked, the twenty-three-year-old shut the door of her bedsit and walked to her local tube station in Hammersmith, but there was a delay on the line and it was past nine o'clock when she arrived at her desk in the War Office. Her boss, Mr Wood, was not impressed, and called out to her impatiently.

'Come along Miss Baker, the Board meeting is about to start! And bring the 'Operation Battenberg' file with you.'

She took the file marked 'Secret' from the security cabinet and hurried along to join the meeting.

Three hours later, after intense discussions in the airless basement room, the meeting ended and Mary escaped into the bright Summer sunshine of St James' Park to eat her lunch. She bought the early edition of the London Evening News, and while she ate her corned beef sandwich she read about the latest Russian who had defected to the UK. It was a time of drama and change, of spies, traitors and double-agents, with the ever-present threat of nuclear war. Mary had been approached by the security services whilst at university and jumped at the chance to work for the Government, using her skills to keep her country safe. She loved her job, although it put a strain on her personal life as she couldn't discuss what she did and often worked unsocial hours. At least with Nigel she could relax, him being in the same trade.

She sighed happily, thinking about him. She'd met the handsome naval officer at work and was immediately attracted by his vibrant personality and good looks – he was thirty years old, tall, dark-haired with lovely blue eyes. She found his attentions irresistible, and soon they were sleeping together. She'd entered the relationship with her eyes open, knowing he was married and had no intention of leaving his wife and young family. During the few months they'd been together she found that the arrangement suited her; she had no wish to settle down, and having a part-time lover worked for her. They were discreet, she enjoyed Nigel's company when he was there, but maintained her independence when he was not. For his part, one could say he was having his cake and eating it.

Mary finished her lunch and returned to her desk where there was a note to say Nigel had called. She rang him back and he said, 'would you like to go to Ronnie Scott's on Wednesday? It's a jazz club in Soho.'

'That would be super!'

'Right, I'll pick you up at 8.'

They had a wonderful evening. They both loved jazz, and the heady mixture of the sound of the saxophone, cigarette smoke and too many gins and tonics put them on a high. They stayed until midnight then fell into a taxi, unable to keep their hands off each other, and spent a night of passion at her place.

The next morning he kissed her, lingeringly, on the lips, then said, 'I'm sorry, I can't see you this weekend - it's our wedding anniversary and I promised Delia I'd take her out for a meal.'

Mary felt a pang of disappointment; this was the downside of the deal, to be expected.

'All right,' she said, 'I could do with some time to myself - I might do some baking.'

On Monday morning, Nigel rang Mary and they met for lunch in a Whitehall pub.

'How was your weekend?' she asked.

'OK thanks, we went to a restaurant near home. But never mind that,' he said, charmingly deflecting the conversation, 'more importantly, did you do any baking?'

In fact, Mary had been called into work for an urgent meeting on Sunday morning but kept that piece of information to herself. She had, however, made time for her hobby in the afternoon so she replied, 'yes, I did, actually. I made a coffee and walnut cake. There's some left if you want to come round tonight…'

Nigel stayed with Mary on Monday night, but then work took over and they were both too busy to meet. Mary was heavily involved in planning for 'Operation Battenberg': her team had been monitoring a suspected Russian agent operating in London and something big was about to break.

Mary didn't speak to Nigel until Friday, when the phone rang at her desk.

'Are you free tonight?'

They met at an Italian restaurant just off the Strand. Nigel was quieter than usual, and Mary wondered whether it was something to do with Delia, but when she asked him he dismissed it out of hand. There were other, more important things on his mind. They finished their main course, then as they ate their tiramisu, he fixed her with his searing blue eyes.

'Look, I've got to go away for a while – can't give you any more details I'm afraid, you know how it is.'

Her heart sank.

'That's a shame – not for too long I hope?'

He glanced away for a moment, unable or unwilling to answer.

'I'm sorry, I can't say. But I will miss you. We've had some good times.'

He took her hands in his and kissed them. This felt like 'goodbye'.

After their meal they went to Mary's place, neither of them wanting to speak, and made love, for what she feared may be the last time. In the morning she got up to see him go and he held her tightly.

'Look after yourself,' she said, tears brimming in her eyes.

'And you.'

'I can't bear that I might never see you again.'

'Never say 'never'!'

As he turned to leave she had a last-minute thought. She dashed to the kitchen cupboard, cut a slice of cake and wrapped it in greaseproof paper.

'Take this! My special chocolate cake.'

He grinned at her – a reassuring, typical Nigel grin.

'Thanks!' he said, and she watched as he put it in his briefcase and went away, down the stairs, finding it hard to accept that this was the end of their affair.

Mary spent the rest of the weekend thinking about Nigel and what he was going to do. He might be joining a ship, or taking up a post abroad, but if so, why the secrecy? But in their line of work nothing could ever be certain, and she had no option but to accept the situation.

On Monday morning she had other matters to occupy her because 'Operation Battenberg' was proceeding apace. Two of her colleagues were following the Russian agent they'd had under surveillance and were planning to apprehend him. Mary was on duty in the radio room where her task was to listen to and transcribe their commentary as they pursued their quarry through the streets of Kensington and into Hyde Park.

'Subject has stopped at a litter bin and retrieved an object – looks like a large envelope,' she scribbled down. 'He's hidden it in the inside pocket of his raincoat.'

The other official added, 'it's a dead letter drop! Got him! We're in pursuit.'

The officers gained speed and caught up with the agent as he reached the Serpentine. Mary was on the edge of her seat as she heard one of them say, 'will you come with us, please, sir? Nice and quietly now. We have some questions to ask you.'

She heard the clink of handcuffs being closed, and after some protestations in Russian the man decided resistance was useless, and submitted to his arrest. Mary and her team were delighted with this result - they knew the agent was passing secret papers to his masters in Moscow, but didn't know who he was getting the information from. Now, caught red handed and in custody, they intended to find out.

The Russian agent was brought to an interview room where Mary was seated discreetly in a corner, ready to take notes of the proceedings. She watched as her boss, Mr Wood, carefully opened the envelope the agent had taken from the litter bin and removed its contents, revealing Top Secret documents, information belonging to the British Government which Russia would find invaluable in its fight against the West. Mr Wood picked up one of the documents, shook off some dark-coloured crumbs and held it at arm's length.

'It's smeared with brown streaks and feels sticky!' he declared, distastefully, then gingerly sniffed the paper.

Mary watched in horror and her blood ran cold as Mr Wood pronounced, 'we don't yet know who is responsible for passing these secrets to the enemy, but one thing's for certain – he likes chocolate cake!'

SELF-ISOLATION

'Come on, Dad, you know it's for the best,' said Adrian. 'You're over seventy, you've got diabetes – you're in the danger zone, you know.'

'Yes…you're right. It's for my own good, and for yours too.'

'It's a nasty old virus and until they've developed a vaccine you can't be too careful. Now, I'll put the newspaper under your door and leave a tray with food outside for you. And you've got the telly in your room, haven't you, and all those DVDs you've been meaning to watch. You'll be fine.'

'Thanks, son. You're good to me.'

The first week passed and father did well.

'I'm quite enjoying it!' he said, speaking from the other side of the door. 'I've read two books and watched a really interesting documentary about elephants – amazing animals. Did you know…?'

Adrian interrupted him.

'That's good, then, Dad, but sorry, I'll have to go now, I've got to get to the shops before everything's gone. It's really weird going shopping now – the town's practically deserted and the people you do see are all wearing facemasks and are scared to speak to each other. You're in the best place, staying in your room.'

'All right, son. Thanks for everything.'

Another week went by, then another, and soon the old man had been in isolation for a month.

'Hope you're not getting fed up with shepherd's pie!' said Adrian, as he took away the half-eaten meal his father had left outside his door.

The old man sounded quite weak.

'No…no,' he replied, huskily, 'I just seem to be losing my appetite a bit…'

'No worries. I'll get you some fish fingers tomorrow. You like those, don't you?'

Another month and Adrian only had to feed his father every other day, he ate so little.

'I'm not feeling terribly well,' he admitted, through the door.

'Don't worry, Dad, just rest. I should have a nap this afternoon, do you good.'

After six months Adrian noticed that his father wasn't eating anything at all, so he stopped feeding him.

A year after the outbreak began, Adrian saw his neighbour.

'How's your Dad?' she asked.

Adrian looked puzzled.

'Who?'

A SPECIAL VISIT TO BATH

June, 1963

Louise, aged thirteen, who lived with her parents in a small village in Devon, showed a sudden interest in going to see her Grandad in Bath.

'Please let me go and stay, Mummy, I'm old enough now!' she implored her mother, Joyce.

'I suppose so, darling – I'm sure Grandad would be very pleased to see you. And this is to do with your project at school, about the Romans?'

'Yes, I'll be able to visit the Roman Baths and do lots of research. Erm…'

She wriggled around in her chair and Joyce waited for her to get to the point.

'Can my friend Jane come with me? She's doing the same project.'

Joyce hesitated. She wasn't too keen on Jane, who was maturing faster than Louise and developing a taste for pop music and boys. She didn't want her daughter to be led astray.

'Oh, please!'

'Well, I'll speak to Grandad and Jane's mother about it and see what they say.'

'Thank you, Mummy!' cried Louise, rather too enthusiastically, and flung her arms around her mother's neck.

The next day, by chance, Joyce met Jane's mother at the local shop.

'I'm pleased I've seen you! Louise has got it into her head to stay with her Grandad in Bath and wants Jane to go with her. Do you know anything about it?'

'Yes, Jane did mention it – something to do with a school project. She seems awfully keen. Would your father mind having two young girls to look after?'

'I've spoken to him and he said it's okay. To be honest, since my mother died I think he's grateful for a diversion. In any case, I know what will happen - he'll make them very welcome, then leave his housekeeper, Mrs Bridge, to do all the work.'

'Poor Mrs Bridge! Well, I have no objection, if it's all right with you. They can catch the train, can't they.'

Jane's mother was pleasant enough, and it seemed a shame to dampen the girls' enthusiasm. Also, on reflection, Joyce felt happier knowing the two were travelling together rather than Louise going alone.

'Very well, we'll tell them they can go, as long as they behave themselves!'

Louise was delighted to learn that Grandad Tom had agreed to have her and Jane to stay for the weekend and the two girls started making plans. The night before they left, Louise carefully packed her suitcase with all she needed, including the pocket money she'd saved up.

On Friday, Joyce met the two straight from school and drove them to Exeter railway station where she bought their tickets and waited with them on the platform. By now both were very excited about their special visit to Bath, and as the train drew into the station Joyce felt a flutter of emotion too, realising that her little girl was growing up and becoming independent. Louise was normally such a quiet thing, but this trip had certainly sparked her interest. The pair climbed aboard with their suitcases, found a seat and waved goodbye as they steamed away, leaving Joyce feeling strangely empty.

As the train gathered speed the girls settled down, grinning at each other.

'Have you got them?' asked Louise.

Jane glanced up at her suitcase on the rack and said, 'yes, of course!'

Two and a half hours later the train arrived at Bath station. Grandad Tom spotted the girls in their school uniforms, greeted them and herded them into his car. As he drove to his home in Weston village, a couple of miles from the city centre, he asked about their journey and plans for the weekend.

'We'll go to the Roman Baths tomorrow, then we can spend Sunday writing up our notes,' said Louise.

Tom was impressed. 'The Baths are interesting – I remember taking your mother there when she was about your age. It will be very useful for your project. Don't drink the water, though – it tastes horrible!'

They arrived at the house where Mrs Bridge welcomed them and showed them to the spare room which they were to share, then gave them supper. It was getting late so the girls went to bed, leaving Tom relaxing in his armchair with a whisky in hand, wondering what his dear wife would have made of it all.

On Saturday morning the girls got up, had breakfast, then caught the bus into the city.

As planned, they spent the morning at the Roman Baths and bought some books in the souvenir shop, then treated themselves to tea at the Old Red House. Louise had been to Bath many times with her parents and enjoyed showing Jane around, but in her friend's company everything seemed different and more exciting. Together they explored record shops and new boutiques, buying trendy clothes which their parents wouldn't approve of.

'Have you had a good day?' asked Tom, as they came in carrying various carrier bags full of goodies.

'Yes!' they said, and went to their room.

Mrs Bridge prepared the evening meal and the girls chatted non-stop throughout. Tom had forgotten how giggly girls could be at that age and was pleased Louise had brought her friend with her, otherwise he wouldn't have had the faintest idea what to do with her. Another early night followed.

The next morning Louise and Jane went for a walk to Victoria Park where the funfair was on, and looked around the stalls. They returned to the house just as Mrs Bridge was about to serve Sunday lunch, but as soon as Louise smelt the food she clutched her stomach and rushed to the toilet where she was violently sick. Shortly afterwards Jane did the same.

'I've got really bad tummy ache!' cried Louise, before rushing off again. Mrs Bridge was worried and called Tom.

'You girls must have caught something nasty! Did you eat anything strange when you were out yesterday?'

'No,' said Louise, 'although…'

'We went to the funfair this morning…' said Jane, sheepishly, 'and we had hot-dogs.'

'Oh, girls!' said Mrs Bridge, 'what a silly thing to do! You should never trust the food you buy at a *funfair*! It could have been hanging around for days!'

Jane had to dash off again and Mrs Bridge said, 'you'd better go to your room and lie down till you feel better. I'll bring you a bucket.'

'And I'll ring Joyce,' said Tom. 'They'd better stay here until they're over it. They won't be able to catch the train home this afternoon in that condition and they'll have to miss school tomorrow.'

On Monday the girls were still poorly and stayed in bed. Tom put his head around the door and they peeked out from under the covers.

'If you're not better by tonight I'll call the doctor.'

'Don't worry, Grandad, we'll be all right by then,' said Louise. 'Tell Mummy not to worry.'

Tom rang Joyce to update her, hoping the girls would be fit to return home the next day. Later, Mrs Bridge took them a light supper on a tray, served her own and Tom's meals then went to her room for a quiet evening while Tom dozed in front of the TV.

Meanwhile Louise and Jane quietly got dressed in the new miniskirts and tops they'd bought on Saturday, sneaked down the stairs and out of the house. They caught the bus into the city and joined the throng of people making a bee-line for the Pavilion, Bath's well-known music venue where many of the new pop groups performed. It was a Monday evening like no other. The June weather was warm, everyone was in high spirits and the atmosphere was electrifying. Louise and Jane joined the queue, shuffling slowly towards the entrance, and showed the precious tickets which Jane had sneakily bought from the record store in Exeter and closely guarded ever since. Pushing their way inside the hall amongst all the other fans they made their way towards the stage, excited fit to burst.

The girls would never have received their parents' permission to attend the concert, and knew they'd be punished when they found out. They also felt guilty for deceiving Grandad Tom and Mrs Bridge, but at that moment they didn't care. All their planning and trickery was worthwhile because, that night, up close, practically within touching distance, they screamed their heads off and got to see The Beatles.

PETER THE PEACOCK

Peter the peacock lived at Corsham Court in Wiltshire with lots of other peacocks and a few humans too. He had a happy life, with plenty to eat and drink and a warm shelter where he slept at nights. Most days he spent his time walking around the pleasant gardens that were his home, admiring the lovely plants and sculptural shapes of the ancient yew trees. The gardens were beautiful, all the year round, and there was always something to see.

Peter enjoyed displaying his colourful, iridescent tail-feathers to the visitors. They took lots of photos of him, but they took photos of the other peacocks too. He was very proud of himself – as befits a peacock – and he wished there was some way he could stand out from the others and be extra special.

Once a week Peter would walk into town to see what was going on. He flew up onto the stone wall surrounding the gardens, hopped down onto the pavement, and strolled into Corsham High Street.

First he came to the Post Office.

'Good morning, Peter,' said the postie as Peter strutted by.

'Good morning,' said Peter.

'Nice day for your walk!'

'Certainly is!'

Peter passed the Town Hall, the jewellers and the flower shop and came to the café with its enticing smell of coffee and bacon sandwiches.

'Good morning, Peter,' said Janet, who ran the cafe. 'My, you're looking handsome today!' she said, admiring his shining blue and green plumage.

'Thank you,' said Peter, fluttering his feathers proudly.

He hurried past the butcher's as it always made him feel nervous, looking at those dead, plucked pheasants and chickens hanging on hooks in the window... But as far as he knew, no one wanted to eat peacocks, so he was quite safe.

Peter walked on down the High Street, saying 'good morning' to everyone he saw, because Corsham is a friendly place. Peter passed the charity shop, the hairdressers and the empty building on the corner where the Bank used to be, then turned into the precinct where there was always something of interest. Today there was a busker playing a guitar, and Peter stood for a while listening to him, nodding his head in time to the music. He hoped the humans would give the musician some money because he played very well.

Peter's favourite shop was the hardware store, which always had lots of interesting products displayed on the pavement outside.

'Good morning, Peter,' said Harry, the owner, who wore a brown shop coat over his clothes. There were all sorts of things for the garden, peanuts and seeds for the wild birds, flowerpots and plants…then Peter noticed something he hadn't seen before: a clear plastic tub full of brown liquid and a label on the side with 'BOOST' written in big blue letters. What was that? He read the label.

BOOST will help your plants grow big and tall and enhance their colours. Make your garden beautiful with BOOST!

This sounded interesting; if it worked for plants, it might work for peacocks, too.

This might be the very thing to make him stand out from the crowd. Peter pecked into the plastic container and sucked out some of the brown liquid. It tasted delicious. He drank a little more…and a little more…and a little more…until it had all gone.

He burped, then suddenly felt the oddest sensation. He looked down at his feet. Before his very eyes, his talons were getting larger, his legs were growing longer and he was getting taller, by the second. He felt his bones cracking and his muscles stretching as his body grew bigger, with new plumage to cover it. His wings became wider, his neck elongated, he could even feel his face creaking and cracking as it grew. Finally, his beak and the crest on the top of his head enlarged. He looked downwards and let out a cry of fright as he saw the ground which was such a long way away it made him feel dizzy. He looked around and found that his head was on a level with the rooftops and his girth filled the shopping precinct.

He heard screaming coming from below, and looked down to see the humans scattering, running away and taking refuge inside the shops. He lowered his long neck and looked through the shop windows where people were cowering with fear at the enormous blue head with huge black eyes, staring at them.

Peter said, 'it's me, Peter the peacock!' but his voice was much louder than usual, an ear-piercing screech, and it only made the humans scream even more.

Peter straightened himself up and with one bound he was back in the High Street. He strode along, looking over the rooftops, noticing parts of the town he'd never seen before. The houses and cars parked in the street were like toys, there for his amusement, and he had fun playing a game, turning over the little vehicles onto their backs with his beak.

One brave lady hurriedly ran to the phone box to dial 999.

'Help, help!' she cried, 'get the police, the fire brigade, everybody you can! There's a giant peacock rampaging around Corsham!'

It was only when several other people rang with the same alert that the emergency services began to take them seriously.

'We'll send help straightaway! And I'll tell the news reporters!' said the Operator.

As he became used to his new size, Peter grew in confidence. He didn't want to scare or hurt people, but he suddenly became aware that he had an extraordinary power. He was a very special peacock – the King of Corsham!

With this thought he fanned out his magnificent tail feathers, filling the whole street with their blues, greens and yellows, displaying the thousand eyes within them. He looked round and saw that the colours were deeper and more vivid than usual, shimmering in the sunshine. He felt prouder than he had ever been. That 'BOOST' had certainly worked!

Peter walked along to the Town Hall and bent down to look through the upstairs windows where the Council were having a meeting. The Councillors blinked with disbelief at the giant eyes glaring at them and ran to the far side of the room as the creature's huge beak poked through, smashing the windows.

With a couple of strides Peter reached Corsham Court where his crest was as high as the chimney pots. He strutted around the grounds, flattening the flower beds and churning up the lawns with his massive claws while the other peacocks stared at him, unable to believe their eyes. He was feeling hungry and in one swoop, seized a sack of peacock food and ate it all himself. His size had given him a ravenous appetite and he returned to the High Street, heading straight to the bakers where he ate all the bread and cakes, then to the café to scoff all the bacon sandwiches.

Suitably refreshed, he made his way to the cricket ground, trampling the grass, knocking over the wicket and sending the players running to the clubhouse for cover. (The match was abandoned, the records stating 'giant peacock stops play'.) Peter burst through the cherry trees bordering the road, stopped for a moment to admire the beautiful architecture of the seventeenth-century Alms Houses with their mullioned windows, then took the path through the trees back to Corsham Court.

His walk wasn't over. He headed to Corsham park, passing St Bart's Church, taking a sideways look at the cock on the weathervane on top of the steeple, then advanced towards the lake, squashing some sheep underfoot as they grazed in the meadow. At the water's edge he jumped in, creating a tidal wave, hurling the fish high into the air. But Peter didn't care about his fellow creatures anymore. Why should he? He could do what he liked. He was the Biggest Peacock in the World!

After his walk Peter felt tired, so he made his way home to Corsham Court where he lay down, tucked his head under his wing, and went to sleep.

*

Meanwhile, Harry, the owner of the hardware shop, realised what had happened and called Mr Singh, the chemist.

'Peter the peacock has drunk a whole tub of 'BOOST' and grown into a giant! Please, please can you find an antidote?'

'I'll try…' said Mr Singh. 'I'll go to my laboratory and see what I can do.'

Armed police and the fire brigade arrived, along with television cameras and news reporters. They quickly surrounded Corsham Court and hid behind the yew trees, staying very quiet while Peter slept. At last, Mr Singh arrived with a large bottle of milky, white fluid.

'I've made up this special formula which makes things smaller. If we can get Peter to drink it he ought to return to his normal size.'

Anxious not to disturb the sleeping giant, Mr Singh crept up and poured the liquid into a large bowl which he left next to Peter, then he joined the other people behind the yew trees, waiting for him to wake up.

At last, Peter stirred. He stretched his legs, spread his wings, extended his neck, and opened his eyes. He was feeling thirsty, and noticed a large bowl of what looked like milk in front of him. He tasted it, and it was delicious. He drank a little more…and a little more…and a little more…until it had all gone.

He burped. Then for the second time that day he felt the oddest sensation. He looked down at his feet. Before his very eyes, his talons were becoming smaller and his legs shorter. His bones cracked and muscles dwindled, his wings and neck contracted, his head, beak and the crest on top shrank, and suddenly he was back down on the ground at his normal height.

There was a collective sigh of relief from behind the yew trees and the police put their weapons away.

Peter looked around him, trying to adjust to his surroundings. His head ached.

'What happened?' he asked, confused.

'You drank too much 'BOOST'!' said Harry. 'Don't do it again! It's not meant for peacocks! And you've got some apologising to do – it's been chaos!'

Peter hung his head in shame.

'I'm really sorry. I had no idea! I promise to make it up to everybody…'

Mr Singh stood back, still concerned, and said, 'I think I should have made the formula a bit stronger.'

'Don't worry, you've done enough,' said Harry. 'The whole town is very grateful to you, Mr Singh.' Then, looking at Peter, he added, 'and so should you be! The trouble you've caused…!'

Peter resumed his normal life, making a special effort to be nice to the humans and to treat his fellow peacocks and other creatures with respect. There was just one thing: even after swallowing Mr Singh's antidote he always remained slightly larger than the other peacocks.

So, when you come to visit Corsham, you might be able to spot him!

ABOUT THE AUTHOR

Originally from Kent, Maggie moved to Bath at the age of eleven and lived and worked in the city for many years.

She is now retired and lives in Wiltshire.

Also available from Amazon:

'When Bombs Fell on Bath'

The first part of the 'Bath at War' Trilogy

Original artwork by Maggie Rayner

Also available from Amazon:

'Bath Ablaze'

The second part of the 'Bath At War' trilogy.

Original artwork by Maggie Rayner

Also available from Amazon:

'After the Bath Blitz'

The third part of the 'Bath At War' trilogy.

Original artwork by Maggie Rayner

Copyright © 2022

Also available from Amazon:

'Moonflight and Other Tales from Wiltshire
and the West'

Moonflight and other Tales from Wiltshire and the West

From the Moonrakers of Wiltshire to the wilds of Exmoor, from sunny Cornish cliffs to a rainy Christmas day in Bristol, these tales will take you on an unexpected journey.

Love, hate, murder.......ghosts from the past and hope for the future.... you will find all these and more in this collection of ten quirky tales. inspired by the West country

Just watch out for the peacocks!

Moonflight and Other Tales from Wiltshire and the West

Maggie Rayner

Original artwork by Maggie Rayner

Copyright © 2020

Printed in Great Britain
by Amazon